Softside

Joseph (Skip) Skibinski

For Josie

Softside

Layout by: James Harley
Cover Design by: Laura Esposito Harley
www.AardvarkWriting.com
Professional writing and design services

Published by Aardvark Publishers
www.AardvarkPublishers.com
Located in the USA
This book was published on-demand by Aardvark Publishers.
Book information and book sales:
Aardvark Publishers
www.AardvarkPublishers.com
orders@aardvarkpublishers.com

ISBN: 978-0-6151-3532-8

Skip and Josie's Wedding Picture

Table of Contents

Foreword 7
Chapter 1   1941 11
Chapter 2   1942 35
Chapter 3   1943 105
Chapter 4   1944 129
Chapter 5   1945 139
Afterword 155

Foreword

I've always heard it said that when someone close to you passes away, it's your memory of that person that keep them alive in your heart. I've always believed that to be true. On November 20, 2005 my father passed away at the age of 87. He left our family with many memories that we cherish; however, the letters in this book reflect a new side, a 'softside' of my father that has become a 'new' memory, a gift from my father that he gave us without knowing it. As you will see, the letters are expressions of the thoughts and feelings of a young soldier about to enter the arena of aerial combat. They are expressions of his deep love for his sweetheart back home combined with his sense of patriotism.

Like many of the men of his generation, these experiences were never shared or talked about. It was over; they served their country and then came home to work and raise their families. World War II veterans are leaving us rapidly, and many are now sharing with us, late in their lives, their memories. There is, indeed, a sense of closure when they talk about these experiences. Finding these letters in my mother's cedar chest inspired me to find out more about the

7

man that I thought I knew. When I told him about the letters, six months before his death, he said "So now you know what I'm really like." And that was it. He didn't seem to want to go further into any discussion. And yet at times he would say – "There are things that I have to tell you." – but we never got to the letters or the past.

And so my sister and I talked about the letters. We knew some of the names mentioned, yet to this day much of the information is obscure and unexplained. After his death, we discovered in his wallet a small photo of what I assumed were members of his flight crew along with a dollar bill that has signatures of men that I thought were his fellow patriots. He held these tokens of brotherhood with him since he returned home from battle. This photo actually provided me with the first clue that I needed to discover more. The name of the B-26 Martin Marauder, Peasapis, became one of my starting points. After hours of Internet searches and e-mails, I was able to find the names of those men who flew three missions on D-day with my father. Two of them, co-pilot Dick Richards and flight engineer, Virgil Jones, are still alive.

Former co-pilot Dick Richards and I talked on the telephone for an hour or so. I was elated to find a link to my father's past;

8

someone who would share with me memories of the man I thought I knew. Dick confirmed that indeed it was Peasapis that he flew with my father on D-Day. He also said that most of their combat missions, 65 to be exact, were flown on a plane called the Pistol Packin' Mama. Dick recounted for me how he and my father earned the Distinguished Flying Cross by crawling into the open bomb bay to dislodge the jammed bombs over open air. He also shared with me how the two of them spent Christmas evening sipping champagne and eating clams over a pot belly stove. Dick said that my father was always the jokester, trying to have fun amidst the seriousness of the war. Dick shared his photographs with me, his links to the past. The photo of my father holding a puppy that he named Buzzbomb, obviously named after the German V-1 rockets, is a reflection of the softside that I never knew. Perhaps these are the stories that my father wanted to share. At the end of our first phone conversation, I told Dick that I know somehow, somewhere, my father knew we were having this talk. It was a 'reunion' that he should have had with Dick that didn't happen in his lifetime but will occur in the 'wild blue yonder.'

Within hours of my first phone conversation with Dick Richards, I also talked with flight engineer Virgil Jones. I was once again amazed and delighted to hear stories and memories of my father. The bond of brotherhood was seared into Virgil's memories and will remain there forever. I will be forever grateful to Dick Richards and Virgil Jones for continuing to share past experiences with me, enabling me to bring closure to my loss.

And so, the letters remain as both a gift and a lesson for us – the power and beauty of a lasting true love.

Joseph Skibinski

Son of Joseph "Skip" Skibinski

Chapter 1
1941

Chapter 1 – 1941

December, 1939

Christmas card, postmarked Braddock

> Merry Christmas Greetings
>
> Wishing you a merry Christmas and a happy New Year
>
> Skip

July 16, 1940

Postcard from Norwalk, Ohio

Hi Jo,

Stopped here for another rest, were jitterbugging with our mothers.

> Zup & Skip

July 16, 1940

Postcard from Norwalk, Ohio

Hi Jo,

So far, so good. Ain't had it so good. Shoot the liquor to me John Boy.

> Skip

Chapter 1 – 1941

June 8, 1941
Fort George G. Meade, MD

Dearest,

Now that I have been in the army for five days, I am in the position to tell you a little more about it.

For the first few days it was really beyond description. It rained for three days and nights. During all that time we had to march and stand around in the rain. It was very uncomfortable. The second day we went through another examination which was very miserable. They gave us an injection against typhoid and from that time on till today my arm still aches.

Yesterday some of my buddies and I were transferred to another unit. We are now in the 176th Infantry – Service Unit – 29th Division. Up to now the Soldiers here are pretty regular. We are now under quarantine for two weeks. Back to tell you how friendly they were the Sgt. and a few Corporals snuck my buddy and I out to the dance on Saturday night. Then things began to happen. That was the first time I've seen a girl since I left you. So you can imagine how much I miss you.

I am writing this letter right after our big parade. It was pretty tough as we had to march in full uniform which weighed about sixty lbs., but it felt like a ton after about ten minutes.

The food out here isn't half bad but if your arms are short you won't get enough. You should have told me a long time ago that you can cook then I would have been eating all I want today.

How's everything at home? How are you? You still love me? You really don't know how much I miss you Oh! If you were only in my arms for at least ten minutes.

Chapter 1 – 1941

Well honey it looks like I'll be home for the Fourth if things don't change. Remember don't make arrangements for that day or the following. By the way I have all weekends off so if you ever get the chance to come out please do.

I'm very sorry I have to close this letter but it's just about ten minutes before taps and I have to be in bed.

Imagine me being in bed at 10:30 and getting up at 5:00 AM not because I like it but I have to.

Yours Forever
Skip

P.S.   Are you sure you stopped biting your nails? How big are they? Will you please send me a couple pictures of yourself at least one big one. You know something to bring back memories. You'll probably ask how much I love you, well I'll answer that now – A Big Two. Don't forget to answer soon. Please address your letters to:

Pvt. Joseph A. Skibinski
Service Co. – 176 Infantry A.P.O. #29
Fort Meade, MD

June 12, 1941
Postcard from Fort George G. Meade, MD

Hi Honey,

Don't let the picture up front fool you. I only danced once since I was here and then I only took five steps and someone tagged me.
D.B.B.
                                                                S.L.M.
Pvt. Skip

Chapter 1 – 1941

June 28, 1941
Fort George G. Meade, MD

Dearest,

I hardly know how to begin this letter, I can't yell at you because you're not here to hear me but when I do get there you'll hear enough of me. In the first place how many times did I tell you not to say how dumb I am. So if you're supposed to put them same words in another letter I'd rather you would not write even though that would make me feel worse than anything.

How do you think I feel with you reminding me of different things how I acted or how I treated you and stuff like that. Don't you think I feel bad enough the way things are now? You say that I wrote to Zup and not to you well I mailed your letter and Zup's at the same time and since then I did not write to no one. I couldn't write as I really was too busy for a week straight now all I have been doing was driving a truck with troops in it from morning till night. It's getting pretty tiresome so today I asked for a transfer to do office work and I stand a good chance of getting in.

About going home for the fourth I don't know definitely yet because we all drew slips and I lost but I went up to the first Sgt. and he said he'd fix me up. If he does not I'm going anyhow. But don't tell anyone about this.

Now I wish you would take a different attitude towards life after all I have to be in here at least one year so why not make the best of it look at the sunny side of the world and you'll always feel better.

Oh yes I almost forgot to tell you yesterday after I finished work they picked me out to box some other fellow. Well you know Skip, he's not so hot but he can take care of himself. I didn't do bad all I got was a cut lip out of the whole affair but I can't tell you whether I won or lost because they do not give no decisions.

16

Chapter 1 – 1941

You talk about me drinking. I didn't have a thing to drink since I got here but that 3% beer and even you could drink that all day. Anyway I'm glad to hear that you're enjoying yourself that's more than I can say.

When I showed your picture to the boys I thought they would go nuts so you better not come out here. I'm afraid I might lose you and that would really hurt. By the way thanks a million for the picture it means more than anything to me. One of the boys even went as far as to write a letter to you and told me to mail it to you. So if you promise not to fall for his line I'll mail it to you in my next letter. It's really sweet I know you'll like it. Don't forget to mail that big picture so I can show them what you really look like and show off a little you know I like that.

Well here I am writing about myself and thinking nothing of it. It's really a terrible thing for me to do you know that I don't like myself. All kidding aside I really miss you. You would probably be surprised how much. It's something more than you can put it words. Still love you and always will. So don't ever start thinking different. Please answer soon.

Forever yours,
Skip

P.S.   Excuse the writing I was in a big hurry. How are Pudgy's nails are they growing any? They better be. Sorry no more space to write so I have to sign off. So long till we meet again.

July 17, 1941
Fort George G. Meade, MD

Dearest,

Received your letter which made me feel like a four star General. Anyway it makes me feel good to know that you think a lot of my writing (or at least you say you do).

Chapter 1 – 1941

I was very disappointed this Sunday. From 10:00 A.M. till 3:00 P.M. I stood out on the highway expecting someone but no one came. So me and my buddy decided to go to the induction center where all the new rookies come in. I met Cuss's cousin out there. His name is Ted. He said hello to Cuss and his family through me because he can't write now as he is supposed to leave for Georgia Monday.

Things out here get better as the days go by. This Thursday we are supposed to go to the gas chamber for a gas mask drill. The officers out here are pretty regular so don't be surprised if I have a few stripes on my shoulder by the fourth. All day Saturday I drove a truck delivering supplies so the day went faster.

How about trying to come out this weekend? If you can't let me know so that I won't expect anyone S.L.M.? I'll tell you what I'll believe you if you can write a letter a little longer than the last one and send me some pictures with it. We are supposed to take some pictures this week so I'll send them out as soon as they are developed. Still love you as much as ever. Only 50 more weeks to go so good-bye for now.

Forever Yours
Skip

P.S.   Don't forget to answer soon and keep your finger out of your mouth.

July 21, 1941
Fort George G. Meade, MD

Dearest,

Arrived safe and sound all in one piece and still thinking of you. One thing I would like to remind you of before I forget is that <u>picture</u>. I was so interested in you I forgot to take it.

Chapter 1 – 1941

Did you hear the President's speech? He's trying to keep us in for more than a year and if that law passes I think I'll give up all hope. To tell you the truth it is taking the heart out of me now.

Well how are you? Did you work hard Sunday? Tell me about yourself. Are you as beautiful as you were? You know I never want you to change. I'm only here one day and miss you terribly already. Forgive the short letter honey but you probably know that I have a lot more letters to write.

As ever,

Skip

July 31, 1941
Fort George G. Meade, MD

Dearest Jo,

Well here it is two months in this place and ten more to go, maybe. Your letter made me feel pretty happy. It's good to know that you think of me.

We pulled in Monday morning at 3:00 A.M. The best part of everything is they only gave us a little sermon and told us not to let it happen again. So you see I'm pretty lucky. It must be that you're my lucky star.

Did Zup go back to work yet? I have no time to write to him now so say hello to him.

You say you're working hard, you're foolish after all those few pennies aren't going to make you rich you know. Anyway I hate to see you work hard, you weren't meant for that. Of course, if I was there I'd help you.

Chapter 1 – 1941

You told me you liked a lot of attention, well you're getting it now honey even if you don't know about it. You should be here to watch the boys admiring your pictures then you'd know.

You'll have to excuse the writing as I am now waiting for payday if I have any left to take. Well not much more to write about except that I still love you, miss you, and always will love you.

Yours forever,
Skip

P.S.:   How about writing a ten page letter honey. Once I start reading I hate to stop. Oh yes, the hair is growing fast. You'd be surprised. I'll probably need a haircut next week. And keep your finger out of your mouth while you're reading this letter at least. Best regards to everyone.

August 12, 1941
Fort George G. Meade, MD

Dearest Josephine,

I really don't even have an idea of how I should begin this letter. If you were in my place I'm sure that you would understand. When I received your letter, card and cigarettes, you wouldn't believe but that was one time in my life when I felt a funny sensation up and down my spine and tears dropping out of my eyes. So you see every time I sat down to get myself to write I couldn't think of words with meaning enough to express my gratitude.

You told me once before how much you love me and that some day I would find out, well I did. You see, you happen to be the only person to remember me on my birthday and that includes all my friends, even Zup and my family. I guess I should be ashamed to say that my family didn't even think about it but maybe I'll feel better if someone else knows.

Chapter 1 – 1941

I suppose I'm boring you to death telling you all my troubles so how about you? How are you? Are you still working? Oh yes and most important of all, do you still love me? I love you and I always will. You see it didn't take me very long to realize what a lovely girl I had and still hope I do. I wish I could see you to tell you how much I really miss you. But I don't know if I'll be down or not. I have a five day pass coming up starting on the 28th of this month so I'll try to see you on Labor Day anyhow even if I don't go home.

Please don't be as negligent as I was in answering your letter. From now on I promise you that your letter will be answered no sooner it gets here.

Forever yours,
Skip

(You're still in my dreams. I give at least a thought every morning and nite. Be good.)

August 22, 1941
Fort George G. Meade, MD

Dearest Josephine,

I regret I couldn't answer your letter sooner but I just got to read it today. You see we go out maneuvering here pretty often and sometimes I'm away from camp three to four days. Josephine if you don't stop treating me so good you'll spoil me and I think I'm getting to be good. Thanks just the same. I want you to know I appreciate what you did for me up till now.

Well I have some news for you. I won't get a leave till after Labor Day, unless someone is willing to take my place up here but I doubt it. So there's no use of crying about if I have to stay I stay and that's that. One thing I'll miss you a lot you know that.

21

It is too bad I can't see you cause I do have a lot to talk about. I spent one day with three British sailors and let me tell you their stories are enough to make tears come out of anyone's eyes. When I see you I'll tell you all about it. For the present it's Cheerio as the English say it.

Forever yours,
Skip

P.S.   Have a good time and don't forget to take good care of yourself. Love me?

September 9, 1941
Fort George G. Meade, MD

Dearest Josephine,

I couldn't write sooner because I didn't have time. We arrived in camp at 7 A.M. and at 9 o'clock we went out for a three day maneuver. It was really tough as we didn't have much sleep or anything.

Did you see Chip around Braddock cause he didn't come back with us and still isn't here?

Did you go back to work yet? Do you feel better? What did the girls at work say?

Well things around here are pretty much the same as they were all except that I miss you more than I ever did. Anyway all of this has to come to an end someday and when it does then I won't have to write to tell you that I miss you cause I'll be right there to tell you.

Please excuse the short letter honey but I really must sign off as I have to get ready for a parade in Washington tomorrow.

Yours forever,
Skip

P.S.   How does Helen feel after the wedding? How's her boyfriend?
Is she still in love? If she is tell her it's bad or she'll lose too much
weight worrying.

September 24, 1941
Wadesboro, NC

Dearest Josephine,

Received your letter Tuesday afternoon and it seems that I
have a little extra time on my hands so I'll tell you more about
everything. The day after I got in camp we all pulled out for Virginia.
We stayed there for one night and five of us drivers pulled out for
North Carolina. Well we got here Wednesday and didn't work very
hard since. We are getting everything set for the rest of the regiment
before they come from Virginia. We will stay here at least till
December sometime. Right now we are only about 800 miles from
home, but it could be worse couldn't it? You asked about the girls
down here. Well I can't tell you much about that as we are about 60
miles away from a big city and that's in S.C. The only girls we see are
a few farmers and all they do is pick cotton from morning till night.
There is really nothing to do here at night no place to go or nothing.
I'm in a bad mood myself today as for the first time in my life I saw a
kid take a fit. We had to put a rifle between his teeth to keep him from
biting his tongue off. I guess it's the change of weather or something
that caused that. Well honey all I can say is keep your chin up, don't
get so cranky and for heaven's sake don't lose your head. Remember I
still love you and always will. And don't forget that date at nine every
night. I'm looking forward to seeing you at Christmas time at least. I

could keep writing but they're calling for me now so be sure and answer soon and don't worry about writing too much you never will.

Yours,
Skip

P.S.   Excuse bad writing and dirty paper as I am dirty right now and am writing this in the truck. Don't forget to answer or I'll bite all of your nails off when I see you. Tell you more in the next letter.

October 1, 1941
Cheraw, SC (Postcard)

Hi Honey,

Still roaming around the country but can't find nothing sweeter than you and I know I won't. S.L.Y.

Skip

Undated, 1941 (in same envelope as the following letter dated November 3)
Bennettsville, S.C.

Dearest Josephine,

I was beginning to believe that you forgot all about me already. I received your letter this morning at 2:30 A.M. It has been laying around at the Morven Post Office for about a week I guess. You see when they change our address like that it takes quite a while for us to get any mail. Right now we don't have much time for anything we go out into the woods for five and half days and then come into camp for Sunday and by then we're pretty well tired to do anything. The only thing that keeps me going is thinking of you. The sooner we do get away from here the better. I do have a lot to tell about what goes on here but it would take too long for me to write that much. Only thing I can say is that I still love you more than I ever did. You asked me about Olga being a bridesmaid well after all you wear the pants in the family so whatever you say is perfectly okay with me. Are you still working? How's everything in Braddock? I haven't even heard from my family yet. Do you miss me honey? I sure hope I'll be able to get home for Christmas anyway. I missed last Xmas Eve with you but I don't want to miss anymore. And do me one favor please. You asked me to be good well I'm doing the best I can so how about you keeping your chin up and smile now and then. Don't be so cranky you only hurt yourself and others by acting that way. How is Zup getting along right now? Are you sure it looks like wedding bells? A good bit of the boys around here are going home and forgetting to come back. Bill will get his discharge by Christmas. Did you see Chip recently? Because they forgot all about him here, he is now considered a deserter. So I guess he'll be in the guardhouse for quite a while when they do get him. Please excuse the writing honey as this is being written about 2:45 A.M. by candlelight. In about a half hour or so we move out into the woods again for another week or so. Please answer soon and don't forget to address my mail to Fort Bragg, NC instead of Morven. Still love me?

Forever yours,
Skip

P.S.   Don't forget them fingernails

November 3, 1941
Bennettsville, S.C.

Dearest Josephine,

Received your letter and it surprised me very much to hear you say that you haven't received any mail from me. I answered your last letter about a week after I sent them cards. For awhile I thought you forgot about me. But then again I don't think you could. It's been so long since I seen you last when I do see you I won't let you out of my sight.

I'm glad to hear that Zup is getting along swell with his girl and I sure am looking forward to being his best man. You sure did surprise me when you wrote me about your brothers. But they better not leave you alone yet at least not until I get there. You're the baby you know and some one has to take care of you. So I have appointed myself for that job. You want me to write a long letter, well sincerely honey there really isn't much to write about. I have been to quite a few big cities here but I'll still take good old Braddock. You can't do much here and to top everything off you can't buy liquor here. I'll bet you like that. I am looking forward to spending this Xmas with you. If anything I'll tell you about everything when I see you. Now you asked for it so here it is; for the next twenty five pages you keep reading I love you I love you I love you etc. and I'll still close with

Love,
Skip

November 11, 1941
Cheraw, SC

Dearest Josephine,

Received your letter and carton of cigarettes for which I thank you from the bottom of my heart. First of all I want to tell you about the weather. In the past few days it got so cold out here we had to put anti-freeze in the trucks to keep them from freezing. When we go to sleep at night we put on all the clothes we have and it's still so cold that you really can't sleep but a couple of hours a night.

You gave me hell for not writing to Zup. Well I did write to him once and didn't get any answers so what's the use of writing. Anyway Zup knows how I feel about writing letters cause he's about the same as me on that point. I did receive a letter from Olga but I

Chapter 1 – 1941

didn't answer it because I lost her address. She must be an interesting sort of person and I am looking forward to meeting her. If I recall correctly the only thing she asked me was how come I don't write to you. Any other person would have asked me the same question I'd have told them to mind their own business but she put it in such a way that I don't believe anybody would get angry.

Well honey tomorrow we pull out for our last maneuver. It's supposed to last sixteen days. After that we are supposed to go back to Fort Meade. You asked me to tell you something about these maneuvers, well I really don't know much. The only thing I do is haul the food out to the troops. As a rule we stay at least about 30 miles from the front line. The only thing we really have to look out for is an airplane attack. When they do spot us they fly down and drop small bags filled with flour so there isn't much danger of getting hurt.

I would like to have Ben and Shatsy's address so I could find out when they are coming home. It would be nice if the whole gang was back at the same time.

We have some pictures taken out here but we sent them out to get them developed. So I'll bring them home with me after all this is over.

You'll have to excuse the writing as my hands are pretty cold so I can't move them around the way they should. It won't be long now but it sure will be good to get back to civilization and you. Till then

Forever yours,
Skip

P.S.   If you don't stop biting those nails I'll have to come back with a nipple for you.

Chapter 1 – 1941

November 14, 1941
Fort Bragg, NC (Postcard)

Dear Josephine,

In addition to the letter I have written you I am letting you know that this is my first time on K.P. since I'm out here. Now when I get back I'll really show you how to scrub pots and pans. Me and Bill are on together and we aren't having such a bad time as we managed to get our bottle of tooth _____ medicine anyway.

Skip
Bill

November 22, 1941
NC

Dearest Jo,

I am answering so many letters I'm running out of words of how to start one. All I can say is that I just about got well when I received your letter. I fell asleep one night and woke up wet, it rained about half of the night. I caught flu in the back the next day. They fed me five pills at one time and taped my back up so after a few days I feel as good as new.

For me this is the night before Thanksgiving. We are celebrating it this Sunday. It is now about 11:00 o'clock Saturday night and the cooks are busy preparing the turkey for tomorrow.

Well the blue army won first part of the war but I don't know what happens next. We are supposed to start fighting again Sunday midnight. As far as I'm concerned the sooner this is over with the sooner I can see you.

Chapter 1 – 1941

I received a letter from my folks at the same time I got your letter and they wrote to me that you were over my place. I'm surprised at you for not telling me nothing about it. After all I expect you to tell me how my mother's taking it more than anyone.

Well it looks like everyone from back home is going to the army. Sometimes I really wonder what is going to become of all this. You tell me they're all taking it hard I don't think they took it as hard as you and I, do you? I think that me and you can find more things to argue about than any two people on this earth, but then they say that true love never runs smooth. Incidentally which reminds me you never told me that you love me in your last letter or do you?

The rumor is that we are supposed to leave this place to go to Fort Meade on December 8th. That means we'll be home for Xmas and there is nothing will make me happier. Tell me something what will you do when you see me now? Probably as usual stand still and turn red in the face. But I won't give you the chance you'll be in my arms before you know it.

Well for now darling you'll have to excuse this handwriting, myself I don't think it's so bad for fire light. Here you got me braggin again. Well when I get up for breakfast I'll look at your picture and say good morning honey. Don't forget I expect an answer if I don't I'll believe you don't love me no more. Do you?

Well I hope to see you Xmas and then we'll make up for lost time up till then. So long.

As ever,
Skip

P.S.   Glad to hear about the nails. You better have some nails cause all mine broke off.

XXXXXXXXXXXXXXXXXXXXXXXXXXXXXXXX

Chapter 1 – 1941

December ?, 1941 (I forgot the date)
Postmarked December 7, South Hill, VA

Dearest Josephine,

Received your letter the same night we started back for Meade, so you see I couldn't answer any sooner. As it is I can't write much now because I don't know how long we will be here. We are about 90 miles from Richmond, VA so I suppose we'll be in Fort Meade by Tuesday.

I received a letter from Ben and he tells me he likes the army. So they finally grabbed Zup too, he didn't even drop me a card to let me know. It looks like there won't be nobody left back home if they keep taking them at the rate they're going now.

I don't know definitely as yet whether I'll be home for Xmas or New Years. I can't get both holidays so I'll have to take what they give me. Anyway if I get Xmas off I'll be home around the 17th or 18th of Dec. If I get New Years I'll be home around the 27th.

Well honey I drove 12 hours so I'm pretty drowsy and I would like to catch a few winks before we start rolling again. We'll make one more stop in Virginia and then straight to Meade. Not much more to say except that I still love you as much as ever.

Yours,
Skip

P.S.   Don't forget to address your letters to Fort Meade, MD from now on. And keep your fingers crossed and maybe they will let me go home Xmas, I hope.

Chapter 1 – 1941

December 14, 1941
Fort George G. Meade, MD

Dearest Josephine,

    I haven't written many letters but of all I have wrote I believe this is the toughest. There just doesn't seem to be anything I can say. If I did I guess it wouldn't do much good. Maybe it's all a dream or something sometimes I wonder. But then again it must be true, you see I may never get the opportunity to look at you admire you and slap your hands again. All of those things seemed to be silly, anyway it's sweet to bring back memories. To be truthful with you I'm just plain disgusted with all of this. All furloughs have been cancelled. In other words we may move any day. As for me the sooner we get this over with the better. Maybe it won't be as bad as it really seems.

    I know you'll raise hell but I'll tell you anyway, when they cancelled the furloughs we sent out for whiskey and drank all night and the next day. There just didn't seem to be anything to save our money for as we can't leave our regimental area. Can't even take clothes to the cleaners.

    Your ears should be ringing I talk to you enough that is to the picture. I never miss saying good morning or good night. Even a few friends that sleep across from me admire you. Well sooner or later things will change for the better I hope. And if I ain't home for Xmas, anyway I still have hopes, you can pretend I'm there that will have to be next best I guess. Still love you and always will. I'm expecting a quick reply.

Always,
Skip

P.S.   I guess your nails are bigger than mine now, anyway they better be.

Chapter 1 – 1941

December 15, 1941
Fort George G. Meade, MD

Dearest Josephine,

I hate to shatter your hopes right from the start but it's pretty definite that I will not be home for Xmas. And I can't say for certain that I'll be there for New Years. Maybe the fellows from Meade are going home but you see we're not from Meade anymore we moved again. We are now guarding the nation's capitol. And the way they tell us it's supposed to be quite an honor. Chips buddy Slim got his furlough you may see him around so he'll be in a position to tell you more about everything. I'm pretty busy now you know how it is when you move. Tell you more the next time. Still love you.

Always,
Skip

My new address:

> Pvt. J. A. Skibinski
> Service Co. 176th Inf.
> Anacosta, DC

New Year's Eve (12/31/41)
Fort George G. Meade, MD

Dearest Josephine,

Received your letter yesterday and I really did expect more hell than you gave me. First of all I want you to know that I am feeling good, right now a few more drinks and I'll be ringing out the old. And if you are not doing likewise it's not my fault. Because I know you can go out if you want to. As to why you didn't get no Xmas present well I lost my whole pay in a crap game trying to make more money to buy something worthwhile. As far as that goes even my mother didn't get anything.

You want me to write you long letters why should when I expect to be home maybe in a few weeks and then I'll tell you all about it. Oh shucks it's no use crying tonight it's New Years Eve and time to be happy even if we're not. Well I got to finish these drinks here and promise not to get drunk no more in the New Year. (I have to tell you right now they are playing In the Mood) Remember?

Aw shucks my mood got the best of me can't write no more even if I tried.

Forever Yours,
Skip

Chapter 2
1942

Chapter 2 – 1942

January 28, 1942
Anacosta, D.C.

Dearest Jo,

Received your letter this morning but I had to wait until this afternoon to answer it. You will have to excuse the writing as this is being written in my truck and my hands are a little chilly. But as I keep writing and thinking of you, no doubt I'll warm up.

First of all I have some good news for you. I will get my second furlough sometime between now and the end of February. Bill is going home this coming Tuesday. I may leave with him and I might not. It all depends when they give it to me.

Surely Butch you're not worried about me going out with that old grandma. If you are well don't. I haven't seen either one of them since I got here, and I don't expect to. I told you I've changed didn't I? And this is one time I mean it.

I want to tell you something Butch and I want you to answer me and tell me what you think of it. I have an opportunity to join the Air Corps. But if I do they don't have the slightest idea where I'll be sent. It may be right here or down to California somewhere. In other words I may bump into Zup and I may not. But to be honest with you I think I'd like flying so let me know what you think about it.

Come to think of it that I.M.Y. you wrote in the last letter couldn't mean I miss you or could it? You know you can't miss me any more than I miss you. I'm afraid that when I do go home you'll have to ask your boss for a week off. I know you won't be in no shape to work. I also kept that date with you Saturday nite. I figured you would get my letter about that time.

You tell your sister Helen anytime she's ready for another boyfriend I'll have one there in a jiffy.

37

Chapter 2 – 1942

I forgot to tell you we are getting some more shots in our arm and they hurt like hell. I have to take two more, but boy I wish it was over with.

Well, I do have some work to do so I'll have to sign off. I know you'll excuse the writing and mistakes as I am writing in a sort of complicated position.

Forever yours,
Skip

Oh yes I forgot to tell you I still love you.　　　SSY

D.Y.L.M.?
I don't suppose I have to tell you about your nails. You know they were really cute the last time.

February 5, 1942
Anacostia, DC

Dearest,

I hope that you will receive my letter this week because I want to live up to my promise. If you don't well don't lose your temper, remember always count till ten. You see I had Tuesday and Wednesday off so I spent the two days taking in the sights. Also saw Sammy Kaye last night. He was okay but he didn't play none of our favorite songs. Maybe he didn't know I was there or he would.

You know Butch since I stopped drinking I'm losing a little weight. I can't figure that out. Maybe it's because I worry so much about you.

Chapter 2 – 1942

You remember Chip don't you, well he got out of the guardhouse and he's back with us now. I don't think he'll ever do something like that again.

Did you notice the difference in the writing honey? Well I'll tell you why, it's because I'm writing with one eye shut. I almost put it out just before I started to write this letter. I was breaking pieces of wood over my knee and a splinter flew up and bruised the white of my eye. The doctor put some kind of salve on then bandaged it up and told me not to move it around.

The weather out here is lousy damp and cold. The only way I can stay warm is think of you. Still love you Butch.

I sure hope you feel better than I do. I'm grouchy as hell lately. Nothing seems to please me here. It's getting late so I'll have to sign off if I want to send this letter tonight.

Love,
Skip

P.S.   You didn't tell me what I.M.Y. means. Did I guess right or didn't I? Love me? S.L.M.

February 14, 1942
7:30 P.M.
Anacostia, DC

Dearest Josephine,

Your eyes didn't deceive you. Bill was home alright but I wasn't. Why I didn't get to go is something I can't answer. But then this is the army so one can expect almost anything.

I have already put in my application for the Air Corps but it hasn't come through as yet. They transferred me into another company. In other words I'm really a soldier now. I am now guarding the Bureau of Engraving and Printing right in Washington. For how long, who knows? Today for the first time in the army I have stood three inspections by two captains and a major. I guess you can imagine the work I had cleaning everything up. If anything it's really teaching me to become a good husband.

You know Butch every picture I get of you, you get more beautiful. In a way it's getting me worried. The first thing I know when I do go home to see you I'll find myself about the tenth in line.

Expect me over either this coming Saturday or Sunday. If I can leave Sat. I'll be home between 12:00 Wed and 1:00 AM. I talked to my first sergeant today about my furlough and he said he was certain I'd get it this coming weekend.

Zup finally loosened up and sent me a card but I lost it and his address was on it so he'll have to wait till I get it somewhere.

Well I'm mad as hell that I didn't get to leave today so I better sign off. I can't write when I'm in a bad mood. If I had your shoulder here to lean on I know it would cure me.

Yours forever
Skip

S.L.Y.
New address

Pvt _____
K Co. 176th Inf.
Anacostia, DC

Figure this out
    IIAYTBMWY
Don't think too hard, it's hard on the brain.

Chapter 2 – 1942

Tuesday Noon (Postmarked March 4, 1942)
Fort Myer, VA

Dearest Josephine,

Excuse dirty paper and bad writing as my hands are filthy.

You'll have to excuse this short letter but I have so much work on my hands that I'm forced to rush this through. As you probably heard I didn't leave till 2:16 Sunday afternoon. I got here just about midnight. Did you have a tough day Sunday? And Jo, I'm sorry you know we promised we wouldn't argue again and we did. It was my fault though, after all that is one of the things they teach us to be on time. If you forgive me I promise you it will never happen again. Love me?

Couldn't answer your letter yesterday cause it took us all day to move. We are now in Fort Myer, Virginia but the address is the same as it was before.

You know I don't want to write anything that would start an argument or make you feel hurt but I will tell you this so that I can get it off of my mind. The memory of that kiss you gave me when you were getting on the streetcar is still lingering on if you know what I mean. Time is flying so I'll have to sign off. I still love you honey. Angry? Be good.

Still in your power
Skip

P.S.   Give my best regards to Olga and the rest of the gang. Send me Olga's address and when I get a little time off I'll drop her a line.

You didn't answer my question in the last letter so I'll ask you again. IIAYTBMWY?

41

Chapter 2 – 1942

Something tells me little Billy[*] would love you to be his mother so you can't say no and break little Billy's heart. Can you?

Were you over my place Sunday after work?

Oh yes tell me what Vince had to say and of course tell you sister I still love her too.

March 5, 1942
Fort Myer, VA

Dearest Josephine,

After this promise me you will never write again about what happened when I was at home. What happened probably happens every day between other people so it must be a sign of true love. If two people didn't care for each other they wouldn't even bother to argue, they would probably laugh it off and forget about each other. Of course you know that is one thing you or I could do. Honey you know darn well that when I told you I was mad at you I was sorry as hell the moment those words left my mouth. In the future I promise it will never happen again.

You say my cousin has a nice boyfriend, darned if I think so. If you noticed anything about him he smokes cigars and doesn't have no teeth to hold them with. I think she can get someone better than he.

I'm off for four hours now that is I have till eight o'clock this evening before I go back on guard. So I spent the time writing letters. I must have written about five and the one that I want to write to I haven't got her address so I can't. I wrote to Zup and asked him all about himself and Francis. When I get an answer from him I'll let you know what he had to say.

---

[*] We can only assume that the name Billy was used to refer to any future children that the couple may have after the war.

Well Butch I don't know when I'll get to see you again things are getting pretty tough out here. They cancelled all furloughs for an indefinite period of time and it's pretty hard to even get a twenty four hour pass. So you must know that I don't have much time to fool around or drink. Well I got to get dressed and go out there for another two hours. So keep writing and be good. S.L.Y.

Forever yours
Skip

P.S.   Don't forget to send Olga's address and if I remember correctly you owe me one stick of gum and one cigarette. And of course you do owe me about 3 months pay. S.L.M. Give my regards to everyone. Tell Mary I'd like to have her give me a few lessons in dancing.

Saturday Evening (Postmarked March 8, 1942)
Washington, DC

Dearest Josephine,

Received your letter right after mess today and it really has me puzzled. You see this is the third letter I am writing to you this week and you turn around and tell me you haven't received a one. I can't figure out how come you didn't get at least one. I purposely mailed the second letter Thursday so that you would get it for the weekend. You see I remember you telling me how much a letter means when you get it over the weekend.

I heard about the big snowfall in Pittsburgh from a few boys who just came off furlough. We didn't have a bit of snow out here. It rained for one day. Today is a beautiful day. Reminds me of the good old summer time and so naturally my thoughts turn to no one but you. Take good care of yourself. I don't want you getting sick. You know your health comes before work. If it was as bad as they tell me you didn't have no business going to work.

About Rats, it's tough being sent away so far. I know you miss him a lot after all he always was a live wire full of pep and always a lot of fun. But to tell you the truth if they would have told me to send my girlfriend's picture back I'd tell them all to go to hell. That is something I wouldn't part with for nobody.

Now that I can't get much time off that is to leave camp I devote most of the time I do have to writing letters. So honey if there's anything you would care to know ask and if I can answer it I'll gladly do so. Oh yes I forgot to tell you I can't leave camp for seven days because my bed wasn't made up this morning. It is a little fault of yours as I dreamt of you and little Billy all night and then got up a little late so I didn't have time to do my work in.

Let me tell you a little about this place and the work we do. We are still sleeping in tents. It really smells up here. You see there was a cavalry outfit up here and they moved but just before we got here. Well what we do is guard all the entrances into camp and also the prisoners. We have about fifty five of them up here. We work in three shifts that gives us two hours on duty and four hours off. The only nice thing about us being up here is the fact that General Marshall lives about a thousand yards away from us. And he is as you probably know a very important personality in this war.

You could send me Vince's address. Who knows if I feel like I do now I'll drop him a line or two also. Or better yet tell Helen to send him my address so that he could write to me and then I'll have something to write about.

Well here I am writing to you about things that probably don't interest you in the least. What I should write about is you and I. Even though I think we understand each other rather well, we should make some sort of plans for the future. This war has got to end some time you know and I'm sure that with you waiting for me I'm bound to be one of those to come back. So remember Butch no more silly arguments of no kind. And please stop asking me if I'm angry, you know I can't be. If I had the time I think I could write a few more pages but I'll have to save them for the next time. I love you and always will. Love me?

Forever yours,
Skip

March 12, 1942
Fort Myer, VA

Dearest Josephine,

Received both of your letters today and sure am glad to hear that you got all my letters. I'm also hoping you receive this letter in a hurry as I have to give it to another fellow to mail for me. I'm on a twenty-four hour post now so I don't even have much time to write. I didn't write to Olga as yet but I promise you I will the first chance I get.

Well honey if you have a chance to come out and see me I think you should jump at it. You know darn well I'll be only to glad to see you. Who knows it may be a long time before I even get to go home again. Please write and let me know when you are coming so that I can tell you how to go about finding me.

One thing I do wish you'd stop doing that is worrying about everything. You know that I love you and I told you that I intend to marry you. So naturally I'll have to get you a ring first. And I promise you you'll get it just as soon as I can afford one. You know darn well what I'm like. Of course I won't be able to afford anything too good but surer than all hell I ain't getting something that's cheap either.

It's a good thing you reminded me about those pictures cause I forgot all about them. I'm tying a string around my finger now so that I'll remember to get them developed.

Honey I've so much to write and for once I really haven't got the time. They're moaning now that I'll be late. I'm hoping this letter reaches you in a hurry so that I can sneak one more for the weekend. S.L.M.

> Forever yours
> Skip

P.S.   How do you like my new handwriting. Oh yes, I still love you. Joke: Hitler pays money for babies but Roosevelt went one better – what did he do?

P.S.   It's 7:40 now & I have until 8:00 to write this so it won't be much but I'll make up for it the next time.

March 13, 1942
Fort Myer, VA

Dearest Josephine,

As you probably know today is Friday the 13th. Supposed to be an unlucky day, but it wasn't for me. I got your package and letter today and boy it was really a honey. I appreciate it very much Butch but honestly you shouldn't have spent so much money. I wish you could have been here to see me when I got your package, the gang around me wouldn't let me go and if you know me you know that my chest really stuck out. When they saw what was in the box they asked me what in the hell did I do to deserve a girlfriend like you. That really did put a lump in my throat because I know I didn't do much. They want your address but I won't give it to them because I'm sure you're busy enough with your work and all let alone writing letters (or maybe I'm jealous).

Chapter 2 – 1942

By the way I'm glad to hear you got a promotion at work even though it carries more responsibilities. However I believe you should ask for a raise because if he put you on that job he knows you must know something about it. Boy, how I wish I was back home now. I'd work 16 hours a day if they asked me to and I do have a lot of things I want to make up to you. You know a few years back I always said that if I ever got married I'd still keep fooling around the way I used to, but I most certainly have changed since then. When we get married you'll have a tough time to chase me out of the house without you. (Unless it's to take little Billy for a walk).

I expect to get a call to go to take my first exam for the Air Corps any day now. So I'm trying to study up a little on the mathematics I've already had. I'm hoping like hell that I can get in because there is much more room for advancement and that means more money. And the sooner I can slip the ring on your finger. Honey they tell me there's a blackout tonight and all the lights will be out in fifteen minutes. If that is true I'll have to stop writing and finish this letter tomorrow. Today was my day off so I went into Anacostia to see if Bob was in the same outfit I am. Well I didn't see him but Bill told me that he is and that he sleeps across from him. So when you come down you won't have much trouble finding me. (I hope you're coming.) You know these beautiful days are getting the best of me. Days like this were meant to be spent with you and not out here. Especially the evenings nice and warm and it's a beautiful sight to watch a soldier strolling down the avenue holding hands. Looking at something like that makes me feel lonesome and blue.

Well no answer from Zup as yet but I should have known better than to expect one. I'm going to try and squeeze in a letter to Vince tonight if the lights don't go out.

Let me know if you received my letter this weekend. I'm hoping you did. Don't forget our date tomorrow night.

Chapter 2 – 1942

What do you mean Shotsy was shellshocked, he didn't see action did he? It's really tough about his brother but I guess something just snaps in your head and you don't know what you're doing. Two days ago a fellow from F Company closed himself in a tent, put the rifle under his chin and pulled the trigger. Fellows tell me there were brains scattered all over the ceiling of the tent. Something tells me that if I didn't have such a wonderful honey to think about I would have went buggy myself. It's so damn monotonous here that if you think about it too much it will eventually get the best of you. Thank your sister for the little letter she sent me. I enjoyed reading it very much. Well honey love you more than ever. I expect to see you soon. Lots of love and kisses.

Forever yours
Skip

P.S.   Don't worry too much and be good. Tell Helen to help you take care of Billy while I'm gone.

March 17, 1942
Fort Myer, VA

Dearest Josephine,

Are you changing or what? After reading this letter of yours I can't figure you out. It seemed so hurried. Just as if you wanted to get it off your mind or something. To tell you the truth it made me feel hurt. What is the matter with you? You must not be the Butch I knew. And of all things you didn't even tell me that you love me. Just wrote down the letters I.L.Y. Of course it may be that I don't rate no more. But if that is so, oh hell let's skip that part of it because it makes me feel bad just to think about it. Forgive me Butch I don't mean to argue with you but it seemed to me as if you have written that letter half heartedly.

Chapter 2 – 1942

I received a letter from Zup Monday. He didn't have much to say but he did say if I answered his letter in a hurry he would write me and tell me something good or rather something that would really interest me. So I answered his letter immediately.

Just because I'm in VA doesn't mean I'm very far from DC. It's only about five miles away from Ann's boyfriend. Cost a dime to get there by bus.

Haven't got much more to write about for I am wondering how I stand. Of course you know I still love you. If I didn't I guess I wouldn't raise so much hell with you. I may as well get this off my mind too. This was the first letter I received from you with one whole side empty and nothing written on it. Still love me?

Forever yours

I hope

Skip

P.S.   You ought to forget different persons opinion of the whole thing and use your own judgment. If I didn't want you to tell me you love me I wouldn't ask you, would I?

March 19, 1942
Fort Myer, VA

Dearest Josephine,

Well here I am, another day another dollar. And perhaps another grey hair. Honey, I'm really sorry I mailed that last letter to you. I should have known that you have troubles enough without me making matters worse. I must have been in one of those moods that day. You probably get that way yourself every now and then. Today I feel pretty good for some reason or other. So I think I'll write a few letters. As you probably know I'm doing so much letter writing lately that it takes up most of my time. And I don't know why but I'm beginning to love it. I got three letters today, yours, Vince's and one from Ben. Vince told me what a grand girl I have but I guess I know that pretty well by now. Judging by the way he wrote my letter, I don't think he is in the least bit shy. He must get that way only when Helen is around. Well love does strange things they say. Hmmmmm we should know. Shouldn't we? I honestly hope that Vince can get a furlough. For his sake and your sister's. I wish we could get together sometime.

I received a seven page letter from Ben but you know what he's like, a lot of B.S. and nothing that's really interesting.

By the way I rushed a letter to Olga. Has she told you anything about it? I meant to tell her to take good care of you and I don't remember whether I did or not.

So honey as a favor to me, for your own good and mine, please stop worrying. It's things like that, that have a lot to do with making you ill. And for heaven's sake quit taking too damn many aspirins they are nothing but a bunch of dope. Well Butch keep a stiff upper lip just remember as I have said before, things like this must have an ending of some sort and I most sincerely hope that that day is near. Here's hoping this letter reaches you before Sunday so that you can have a more enjoyable weekend. Remember a good old timer – "When your hair has turned to silver" well I'll still keep on loving you not the same but more as the days go by. I love you. S.L.M.

Forever yours
Skip

P.S.   Ben told me in his letter that Shotsy is in the Pacific Ocean somewhere, so I don't know who to believe. Please don't call yourself bad names like D.B.B. You're beautiful to even be thinking such things. Still love you.

Chapter 2 – 1942

March 25, 1942
(no envelope)

Dearest Josephine,

I sure hate to disappoint you but the way things stand now it doesn't look like I'll be home for Easter. Asking for a three day pass right now is just like asking for a discharge. Of course a few of the boys will get to go but us Yankees haven't got a chance. So there is nothing we can do about it but grin and bear it. So the only chance I'll get to see you is when you come out here. Are you sure of coming out Friday after Easter? If you are I'll make it my business to get a few days off. You and Ann will probably go where Bob's at first and I'm certain he knows how to get to where I'm at. I don't now whether you'll like Washington or not. As for myself I don't think so much of the place.

Got a letter from Zup today. Boy he must be getting classy as all hell. He uses Hotel stationary and sends his letters air mail. He didn't have much news. Just talked over old times with me and telling me how swell it would be if we could get together. Who knows, someday we may. He tells me he isn't engaged to Frances and I believe him. I think he'd tell me the truth if anybody. Well Butch it's time I signed off and went to bed. Let me know when to expect you. I'll be waiting patiently till then.

Forever yours,
Skip

P.S.   Vince doesn't have much to say in his letters regarding you girls. If he did I don't know whether or not I'd tell you. Ha Ha. Strictly between us means you understand don't you. I will tell you this much over and over again. I still love you.

Chapter 2 – 1942

March 31, 1942
(Payday)

Dearest Josephine,

It seemed like ages since I heard from you last. It must have been at least three or four days. I was beginning to worry about you. I've received three letters before I got yours from Zup, Vince and Ben but I didn't answer any of them because I was wondering what happened to you. Well honey I positively will not be home for Easter. And believe me it hurts me as much as it does you, if not more. One thing I do want you to do for me Easter that is say a little prayer, it might help. Of course I want you to stop in and see my people also.

Honey the best way you can come out is by train; it may cost a few pennies more but it's worth it. If possible try to get a train that goes straight through so that you won't have to transfer.

Before you leave write me and let me know what time you are supposed to arrive and I think I can arrange to meet you at the Union Station in Washington and from there we can go and see Bob in Anacostia.

You can probably tell by the writing that I'm mad as hell and I am, here it is payday and I can't even get a pass to go to town to buy my honey a card or something. So I've decided to drink a little right here and play some cards. They're waiting on me now. But before I go broke I'm sending you a few bucks to get yourself a box of candy or something. I may not get another chance to write before Easter so if I don't I hope you have a wonderful time and the best of everything. Still love you as much as ever.

Forever yours
Skip

P.S.   If you don't get an Easter card forgive me but that will mean that I couldn't go to town to get one. I will try to get someone to buy a few for me. Explain to my friends. Can't wait till I get to see you. I wish tomorrow was Friday after Easter.

Skip

April 6, 1942
Fort Myer, VA

Dearest Josephine,

It sure seems like we get all of the bad breaks don't we? First I can't come for Easter and then you can't come. Well I'm sorry as hell you can't make it you're really missing something. I wish you could stroll through any park here with the Korean cherry blossom trees in full bloom. It's really nice. I have off this evening and that's just where I'm going. Pick myself out a nice bench and sit down and reminisce a little.

We're going on maneuvers also but we'll join them out there April 20, and before we go I understand everyone has to get a five day furlough or a three day pass. So it looks like I'll see you in the near future.

I'm glad to hear you had a good time Easter cause we didn't do so bad. Six of us drank 4 quarts of liquor. We got so drunk they chased us off the drill field and told us to sleep it off.

Well honey the bugle just blew first call. I only have a few minutes. So till I see you (I hope) remember I still love you.

Forever yours
Skip

P.S.   They think they did us a hell of a big favor by doing away with postage stamps.

Chapter 2 – 1942

April 13, 1942
Fort Myer, VA

Dearest,

I'm not in the least bit surprised that my letters were mixed up. You see I've had so much on mind that I didn't know whether I was coming or going. I'll bet I've aged ten years in the last few days. Now I'll tell you why. Just as I was writing to you and Mom the last time a Corporal from headquarters comes in and notifies me that I must appear Monday morning for my final physical and mental examinations. Well it really upset me a lot. As I have written I was pretty well under the weather Sunday so there was some doubt in my mind as to passing the physical let alone the mental. For fear of not passing either test is one of the reasons I didn't tell you about it in the last letter. But now that this terrible ordeal is over with I'm happy to say I passed both tests with a very reasonable grade. I have but one final thing to do and that is to go before the Board of Examiners which will take place sometime this week. And if they don't pass me, well at least I'll know it's not on my part. On the other hand if they do pass me (which I sincerely hope) it won't be long before I'll be in the Air Corps. I'm told I'll be sent to Maxwell Field, Alabama for my eight month training course. If I complete this course satisfactorily I'll be automatically commissioned a second lieutenant drawing a pay of $245 per month plus $150 clothing allowance (Not bad is it?) Maybe I'm crossing my bridges before I get there, but as you probably know I am an aggressive type of person, and if the Board passes me I'm sure I'll make the grade.

The beauty part of it is before I do leave I will get at least a two week furlough (Imagine two whole weeks with my honey). That will be something to take down to Alabama with myself. Of course the whole affair has its bad points also. For instance, leaving and not knowing whether there will be a return trip or not.

Chapter 2 – 1942

I know for a fact, or at least I'm pretty sure I did this against your wishes as much as Mom's but I think it's best for me. And Honey if you believe me and trust me I'll make it my business not to fail you.

I think that's about enough about myself. Tell me how are you? Write me more about yourself honey. I am interested in my friends also but not half as much as I am in you. How is Billy? You know it's stupid of me. I didn't inquire about him for a long time (and I'm supposed to be his Daddy).

By the way, how is Vince? I don't remember who wrote last him or I.

Well Butch I've had a pretty tough day of it so I think I'll get a real night's sleep. It will be a goodnight's sleep if I dream of you and I'm sure I will.

Forever yours
Skip

P.S. I suppose you know I love you more than ever. Please don't mention things to me that I've said before and didn't mean. You know I regret it till this day. From now on I don't want to hear the word <u>hate</u> mentioned between us unless you really mean it. Please don't.

June 4, 1942
Washington, DC

Dearest Josephine,

Just letting you know that I've arrived safely. On the other hand as to my health I don't feel any too good. Caught a terrible cold on the way over, take that and put it together with heart trouble it adds up to enough to depress anyone. You know you do have the biggest part of my heart (what's left is with me) so take good care of it.

I don't know how long I'll be stationed here before I'm sent away so just mail your letters to the old address. I may remain here a few days or months.

Tell the Gold dust twins I'll drop them a line when I get situated. Well darling things are moving pretty fast around here right now so I'll have to sign off. Here's hoping you will always love me as you have. And if at all possible I would send you the little part of my heart I do have left with me.

Forever yours
Skip

P.S.   I'm glad you took my departure like a trooper and didn't let a tear drop fall. It made it so much easier for me you know.

Love you 2-1/2

June 8, 1942
Fort Myer, VA

Dearest Jo,

Well I see you're as bad as I am, you write a letter and then tear it up. In a way I don't think it's right. After all there shouldn't be any secrets between us if we love each other. You want to know what makes me act the way I do well I'll tell you. If you remember correctly, a year ago when I was inducted into the army I swore I wouldn't get married till I got out. All of that brings us down to the point of me giving you a ring. Because if I did that I wouldn't expect you to go out with nobody. And you know darn well I think too much of you to deprive you of a good time So for our own good I think we better forget about things like that until this mess is all over with.

Chapter 2 – 1942

And by the time this is over it may take years. During that time you may fall in love with someone else. That would hurt very much but they say that good old father time is the best cure for anything.

Vince and I did meet a couple girls on the train who were from Ohio. They were vacationing and I talked them into staying in Washington for one day. Naturally with my gift to gab and their money we had a pretty good time. I told one of them something about writing you a letter. I wonder if she did. Did she?

Well honey you can write me and give me your opinion of this affair. You know I still love you and always will be

Forever yours,
Skip

Saturday (Postmarked June 15, 1942)
Fort Myer, VA

Dear Josephine,

Well I am certainly glad to find out what you really think of me. And thinking what you do of me you can't possibly love me. I agree with you on every point, I'm strictly no good, a damn louse if there ever was one. I will tell you this much though, many a time I have tried to change my ways only to fall back down again. As sweet as you are you deserve much better treatment than I have given you. But on the other hand don't get swell headed. Everyone has some bad points and you have too. For instance if we two should get married you probably wouldn't let me out of your sight for 15 minutes without knowing where I was at. I'll agree with you every man loves attention but there is such a thing as overdoing anything. The thing that makes me angrier than hell is when you tell me I tried to make a fool out of you. You know damn well if I didn't care for you I wouldn't have spent any time at all with you. And you know that I wasn't trying to force myself upon you. If that was the reason I would have given up a long time ago.

Anyway let's quit arguing for awhile, we do enough of that when I'm at home. And who knows maybe I'll wisen up. If you don't want to write well I guess I can't force you to. But I would like you to send me Vince's address as I have lost it, or is that asking too much?

Now come on I want to see you get up on the right side of the bed for a change and you'll find that you will feel much better. You always look at the wrong side of life. And I wouldn't want you to get gray hair yet. So take good care of yourself.

With love,
Skip

P.S.   Not that I'm jealous but I wish you wouldn't tell me where you go or who you go out with I'm not interested. Mad?

2-1/3

Postmarked June 19, 1942
Fort Myer, VA

Dear Jo,

I hardly know what to write. Everything is so damn quiet here it ain't even funny. You ask me to try and come home, what do you think I am a general's son or something. Anyway everytime I do come home I do nothing but cause a hell of a lot of misery and worry for my people and everybody else. At least if I do something wrong out here nobody knows anything.

Well how are things with you Butch? You shouldn't complain about the weather what will you do when winter sets in?

Yes I'm still loafing. You know me lazy as hell, no ambition whatsoever! Yes Dear 2-1/2.

Love
Skip

P.S.   See Pvt. Buckaroo with Andrew Sisters. Lots of good songs in the picture.

June 25, 1942
Jefferson Barracks, MO

Dear Jo,

Couldn't answer your letter sooner cause I was really in a mess, packing up and moving. I should tell you about the trip but I can't because I traveled first class Pullman and slept most of the way. This is a wonderful spot. Nothing to do but go to school. I expect to stay here at least six weeks after that, who knows. This place is only 10 miles out of St. Louis but I haven't been to town as yet so I don't know what it's like. Have to sign off as I have my hands full at the present and I'll let you know more the next time.

Love
Skip   2-1/2

Postmarked June 30, 1942
Jefferson Barracks, MO

Dearest Josephine,

Well miracles do occur, you still remember me. How do you do? No Dear, I didn't get the other letter but I suppose it will be sent to me within a few days.

Chapter 2 – 1942

As I have written before I can't tell you much about the trip as I slept most of the way. I can write and tell you a little about this camp though. First of all it's hot as hell, only 104 in the shade. We're situated on a little hill just along the muddy Mississippi just about 10 miles down from the city of St. Louis. Last Saturday I went into St. Louis and I felt right at home. It's every bit as smoky and dirty as Pittsburgh.

Incidentally Butch you can address your school boy as Cadet, not that I'm trying to brag but it is supposed to be an honor. Not that I'll make the grade but I'll at least have the satisfaction of having made a good attempt. You have probably seen pictures of West Point Cadets in the movies well we run things on the same basis such as no smoking or drinking on school days. All this is based on the honor system. The school schedule is really tough and you may or not be interested but here is the schedule.

9:00 – 9:25	-	Aircraft Engines
9:30 – 9:55	-	Instruments
10:00 – 10:25	-	Props, Hydraulics & Starters
10:30 – 10:55	-	Meteorology
11:00 – 11:25	-	Navigation
11:30 – 11:55	-	Code
1:30 – 1:55	-	Supply and Administration
2:00 – 2:25	-	Theory of Flight
2:30 – 2:55	-	Chemical Warfare
3:00 – 3:25	-	Int. Code
3:30 – 3:55	-	Law (Military)

That's eleven subjects with only a half hour of school time for each one. Naturally that means a hell of lot of studying after school. This is only preliminary training. I dread to think of what the next course will consist.

But then again there is a brighter side to all of this. It's every bit as elaborate as they claim. We are set aside completely from the rest of the army and (up to now) considered as future officers. We also have priority on everything here; such as food, we get milk and ice cream 3 times daily the others once. They hold special dances for Cadets only and they tell us that only the cream of the crop attend these. Of course I have never as yet attended one of these affairs as I'm not here a week yet. In the future I may be able to write you more about these shindigs. We have three days a week off that is Wednesday, Saturday and Sunday. By this time you should be so bored that you'll fall asleep without any trouble. I thank you for wishing me a lot of luck no doubt I'll need it. Anyway if I do wash out as a pilot, navigator or bombardier I can always become a rear gunner.

As for the pictures they are getting developed now. Will send you some when they are ready. Bought a fairly good camera and I would like to snap loads of pictures here but they won't permit me to do so.

Miss you a lot but I will attempt to make up for it when I do see you again (If I get to see you). One never knows does one. Well Butch with you rooting for me I'll at least make a damn good try.

Love   2-1/2
Skip

P.S.   The reason I wanted Vince's address was to get an address from him of the girls we met on the train but she wrote to me so I didn't bother writing to Vince. Tell the Gold Dust Twins I would like to have some of that flying fudge or whatever they call it.

(This should be long enough)   Love me?
Prove it, show me
I'm from Missouri

Chapter 2 – 1942

2 July 42
Air Corp time = 21:18 (9:18 PM)
Jefferson Barracks, MO

Dear Jo,

I'm sure I'll receive your letter tomorrow but with an exam coming up this weekend I wouldn't have the time or energy to answer it. So I decided to drop you a few lines tonight.

Well we attended one of those parties I wrote you about yesterday. I had a wonderful time but tonight I'm beginning to wonder if it was worth it. (A day of study to catch up on). They didn't serve nothing stronger than punch. You could have danced inside or out on the terrace (just like Bill Greens). Oh yes, we were given dancing instructions by a well known dancing team so I'm warning you now you'd better study up on your Rumba and Tango because a few more parties and I'll be an expert (braggin again).

The pictures won't be developed until next week so you'll just have to have a little patience. Did I tell you about that killer diller haircut they make us get? Well it's just like the last one I had only a little shorter.

Before I fade away I want to write and tell you the way the upper classmen initiated me today. I sat down to eat dinner and while eating we were doing a lot of B.S.ing Somebody pulled off a joke so naturally I laughed. The Cadet sitting across, being an upper classman, told me to wipe that smile off and set it on the table. So I took my hand wiped it off and placed it on the table. As I placed it I laughed again. Then he told me to wipe this smile off with the other hand and march both smiles clear around the table. So with both hands (my smiles in my hands) I marched around the table. When I placed them down this trip I made sure I didn't laugh again.

It's a hell of a lot of fun, just like college.

Well Butch as we say in the Air Corps I must get on the beam and do some studying. So that I can do some more traveling (I hope). So long Butch and don't pick up any wooden nickels.

Love   2-1/2

Skip

---

8 June 1942 (Postmarked July 9)

Dear Jo,

Happy to say that your school boy is coming along in tip top shape – that is up to the present time. This course will be over in a few weeks time and that means some more traveling pretty soon. Some fun – eh!

You ask me if I miss you or home, to be frank with you it seems that I don't or at least not as much as I used to. I don't know whether the activities here have anything to do with that or knowing that I can't get home or then again maybe it's because I haven't got as much time as I've had before.

I'm sending you a few snapshots. They're not so hot but all the others were pretty bad so I sent them home. Just as soon as they issue us our Cadet uniform I'll take a few more snapshots. I'm sure you'll love them – the uniform.

There has been a slight change in address, my error, that's why your mail is getting here about a day late. It's the 28th Tech Sch Sqd. instead of 26th.

I don't want to make any future promises but there is a rumor that after finishing this school we may get another furlough as the other schools are still filled up. (not certain).

Oh yes I don't know whether you listened to the radio or not. We were on a coast to coast hook up Tues Eve for a half hour, singing songs. Still in class eh!

So be good and don't worry too much. It's hard on the brain.

Love,
Skip

P.S.   Received a letter from the girl we met on the train. She's from Ohio. So I'm sure you'll excuse me for shortening this letter so that I can send her a little B.S.

---

10 July 42
Jefferson Barracks, MO

Dear Jo,

Why I decided to write, I don't know. Maybe it's because I have you on my mind. Anyway, in about an hour or so we are leaving for Lambert Field to see an Air Show. I could probably write a lot more after I've seen it but then I may not have the time when I get back. Things look good the whole group of other boys that were here and went to a different school all got a 40 day furlough. You know that won't make me mad.

What you know Jo? Still eating as much as ever? You know I don't have no one to bring me a glass of water. I sort of miss that.

It's getting time to leave so I'll have to sign off.

Love, Skip   2-1/2

Chapter 2 – 1942

14 July 1942
Jefferson Barracks, MO

Dear Jo,

An appropriate beginning to a letter to be written to you is something very rare. I would venture to say that I love you but unless my imagination is running away with me something is definitely wrong thereby leading me to believe that I haven't the right to do so. Although I may have been a little lax in my last few letters, I have tried in my very best way – which in all probability wasn't good enough for you – to let you know the routine I'm going through. No doubt it was all dry stuff not worthwhile reading, but I'm in love with it which makes it so much easier to put my whole heart and soul into it.

So if it isn't too much effort on your part, a reply to at least one of my three letters will be most humbly appreciated. On the other hand if your attitude has taken such a terrific change toward me I'd rather you didn't answer. If I'm making a mountain out of a mole hill I know you'll disregard this letter completely.

Love
Skip

---

16 July 1942
Jefferson Barracks, MO

Dear Jo,

By this time you are no doubt wondering what in the _____ has got into me to send you a letter as I have. Truthfully I was beginning to believe that you have forgotten me. Stupid of me wasn't it? In the future I won't allow my temper to get the best of me.

Chapter 2 – 1942

As for the package which you have sent me, I'm certain that you'll understand what I mean when I say that words cannot be found to show my appreciation. I detest the thought of thinking that you have deprived yourself of something in order to send me the pkg. Butch, your life is no bed of roses, so have all the fun you can for who knows what tomorrow will bring!!

With everyone at home it is a shame I can't get at least three days off. As you know this is the last week of school and with a shipping list being made up I can't afford to be away from here.

I ran into Pummy's younger brother in St. Louis last Sunday afternoon and bumped into him again out in Forest Park the same evening. I didn't spend much time with him as he met a girl and dated her up well three's a crowd.

They sure have us humping around here the last few days. We're supposed to be inspected by some General so I'll have to get to work.

Love
Skip

P.S.   Happy to hear you got better working hours, that should give you more time to go out and enjoy yourself.

---

22 July 1942
Jefferson Barracks, MO

Dear Jo,

According to all the latest rumors, which were supposed to have originated from a very reliable source, we will move within seven days. You asked where to .....Your guess is as good as mine.... Personally I hope it's Santa Ana, 30 miles away from Zup. Haven't seen the kid for quite some time now, sure would be good to bump into him somewhere.

At the present we are doing nothing. School is out. That gives us a few days of relaxation. Have arrangements made to take a trip down the Mississippi on the S.S.Admiral sometime this week. Ought to be some fun dancing, swimming right on the boat.

Still the same old Butch aren't you, letting your temper get the best of you...I thought you reformed by now.

We got a little action the other day, while parading 240 men passed out like flies, seven of them layed down for good, but as they say the show must go on.

If I wrote any more it would have to be a pack of lies so to remain on the honest side I'll sign off.

Love
Skip

P.S.   Sometimes I wish there was a little Billy back home. But as things stand, in the long run you'd be sorry so perhaps it's better the way it is.

Aug. 14, 1942
Jefferson Barracks, MO

Dear Josephine,

Maybe I should attempt to give an excuse for not answering your letter sooner – you have been so antagonistic lately I don't know whether it would do any good to even try. Why you always insist on looking at the wrong end of things is something I can't understand. As I have said before, you let your temper get ahead of you – and believe me if you want to you can have one that's enough for the two of us to

Chapter 2 – 1942

handle. As for my letters well maybe I could write a flowery epistle just like the next fellow – If I thought it might help, I would. Surely, you don't think that I could forget you so easily!! From your letter I take it for granted that I should inquire as to where you go – with whom and why. You also stressed the point that I'm not interested – you know I am, more than you think! My reason for not asking, very simple, -- From the time I have known and spent with you, I'm truly proud to say that wherever you go or whatever you do you can take damn good care of yourself. (Don't weaken). It is one of the many things I love you for. I realize that it isn't too easy back home – wondering and worrying about someone you really care for. Don't you think the same goes on here but if we took it too hard you know what would happen. All this school and studying is nerve racking enough.

Getting back to us – I believe something should be done to remedy that little something that seems to be standing between us. So, if you have any suggestions to make please write and tell me, you know I'm more than willing to meet you halfway. If there is anything in particular you'd care to have me write about let me know. I know that you are rather emotional and love attention also perhaps a little forgetful so in the future I shall constantly keep trying to knock it into that beautiful head of yours that I love you. I honestly hope the feeling is mutual. And Butch I do have a good reason for not writing. I wasn't going to tell you why but ---- Oh well perhaps it's because you're different from the rest. We've had our stuff packed for one solid week, ready to get on the train and go to Alabama. Yesterday we suddenly got word that the school from there has been moved to Nashville – I suppose we'll wait some more.

How about yourself honey? Still kicking everything around? You know I haven't got a snapshot of you for sometime. I know you're getting prettier by the day. Don't you think that's reason enough to send me one. With everyone in the army I guess there isn't much doing back home is there You can see by the writing that I've written this under extremely poor conditions – under our street light at

11:45 PM. Hold everything now don't get excited there is still a little space and time left so I can remind you once more – I love you.

Love
Skip

P.S.   Can't resist telling you that within a week or so I'll be able to put a part in my hair -- If I'm not forced to get it cut in the meantime.

Aug 22, 1942
Jefferson Barracks, MO

Dearest Jo,

For a half hour now I have pondered on how to begin this letter – it's no use I could think from now until dooms day, without success. You're so honest and sincere in everything you do – well, you make me feel like a cad. How can I express my appreciation? – I will say I'm grateful for everything and if it were at all possible to love you any more – you know I would.

By looking at the clipping I'm mailing, you can see that I have crashed the society circle here in St. Louis. Only one error – I'm not a Sergeant – it's a borrowed shirt. I'm officially a cadet. Just couldn't resist the temptation of showing off a little. You don't blame me do you? The picture was taken at the National Catholic Youth Convention in the Hotel Coronado. Strictly formal.

And Butch, before you draw any conclusions you know that all these girls are nothing but a passing fancy. You know I must have some recreation – but that's as far as it goes. They aren't so bad but just looking at your picture puts them to shame. Placing you among these girls would be just like putting in a lake in the Sahara Desert. So different, beautiful that you couldn't help but stand out.

Chapter 2 – 1942

I've asked you so many questions in my last letter dear – to which I haven't received any answers. Not holding out on me – are you?

I received a letter from Zup today. He tells me it won't be long before he goes over the pond. He claims you write to him daily – Right? Daily and me weekly I can't believe it. Not my honey, I come first.

What is your opinion of this whole mess at the present dear? Do you think I'll get another leave before this is all over with? Just curious as to what you think, so remember I want to hear more about yourself in the future. After all that's all I'm interested in.

I inquired in my last letter if there was anything I could do for you? – No reply – How come? Just visualize me in your parlor with my arms about you planting a kiss on that pert little nose of yours – You would speak to me truthfully then. Well that's just the way I expect you to write. I'm expecting to put this pen to a lot of use – nothing but writing letters to you. Remember, I'm still the guy who loves you.

Love
Skip

P.S.   Forgot to tell you – spent Saturday eve at our Opera – my first time. Imagine me at an opera for the first time and it had to be one of the biggest in the country the Open 'Air Municipal Opera – the production – Show Boat. Enjoyed it tremendously but I missed you like nobody's business. Once again (just to remind you)

Love
Skip

Chapter 2 – 1942

Sept. 3, 1942
Jefferson Barracks, MO

Dearest Jo,

Forgive me for not answering your letter sooner dear but for a minute it looked as though I would be able to surprise you. You see I've been working on a furlough all week and I thought sure as hell I'd get it. I had a fairly good reason for one – I don't know whether you have heard or not but my sister is ill. Anyway I found out this morning that I couldn't get it. So you can see there isn't much chance of seeing you for quite some time.

The pictures were swell honey. You really look good. But I don't believe the camera did you justice. I sure hope you get a better job but before you start on your new job don't you think it would be a good idea to take a good vacation – Of course so you could come and see me or rather so I could admire you personally. Haven't did that for a long time now.

Honey I hate like hell to end this letter so abruptly but my dinner hour is about up. So I must go back to school. If I don't learning nothing this afternoon I shall blame you as my thoughts will be with you.

Love,
Skip

P.S. Do you have to be so stubborn – must you wait to get a letter from me before you write – or aren't you convinced that I love you. I'll soon have a few more pictures I'll send and I don't want you telling me I'm a show off because I'm not still mad? Well you look pretty when you are, makes me love you much more.

Love,
Skip

Chapter 2 – 1942

Sept. 10, 1942
Jefferson Barracks, MO

Dearest Jo,

What in the world ever gave you the idea that I don't care to receive more than one letter a week from you? If it was at all within my power to do so – I'd order you to write me daily. Being a young lady – a beautiful Miss at that – you know there's nothing more a fellow craves than a little encouragement and attention from the fairer sex – especially someone he really cares for. Undoubtedly it is rather hard to write to the same person day in and out – but remember a few lines now and then really hit the spot. Take two persons in love – words are of no avail – that golden silence seems to take care of everything. We two being so far apart that is bodily – must be thankful that we can at least correspond with each other reminding ourselves that our hearts are still in the right place.

Honey I've told you a million and one times if I told you once that if you keep eating the way you have been, you'll get sick. It's a wonder you didn't take ill a long time ago. The pity of it is I couldn't be there to hold your hand – I'm sure that would help a little. You know Dear, you take sick and I sprain an ankle – playing basketball. But I haven't told you – I've been elected Capt. of the team out here and up to the present we're doing alright. And Dear – I'm not bragging, merely stating facts.

Makes me very happy to hear that you're having some fun Butch. Believe me, never pass up a good time – you only live once you know. That is not ordering my honey to go out and fall in love with everyone – You leave your heart strictly with me, I'll take good care of that. Now let me tell you of my weekend adventure. Spent it with a Miss Hope out at her home in Crystal City. It's a wonderful little place – homes built on the same order – beautiful bungalows (that's for us). Saturday eve we dined and danced at a place called Black Forest – it really puts Bill Green's to shame in everything but the music. Sunday was a basket picnic affair which took in swimming and horseback riding. All in one it was a pretty swell affair. And you know Dear if you were there it would have been perfect.

Well Butch this letter has taken up two of my classes now. Do you think I should continue to answer your letters in school? It's so quiet then my thoughts are even more so with you than at other times. Look Dear I can't have a sick girl on my hands so you just have to get well – And I'm hoping this letter will aid you in doing so.

Love,
Skip

Reminders of the Day!!
>   I love you
>   Keep your finger _____
>   Be good

Sept. 15, 1942
Nashville, TN

Dearest Jo,

Yes, I've moved again – down south a little way – Tennessee. Never a dull moment, that's the army for you. The only thing that really hurts – I'll have to ask you not to write, as we have no mailing address as yet. I do know that the camp is situated about five miles out of the city of Nashville. I can't say much more as I haven't seen anything or did anything yet.

If you don't hear from me for about a week don't be alarmed – within a week I may ship elsewhere. So rest your arm up dear for when I do ask you to write. I'm going to really expect a letter. Love you Dear, but I don't intend to come home till your nails are at least half an inch long.

Love,
Skip

P.S. Kindly inform my people as tomorrow I may not have the time to write.

Sept. 19, 1942
Nashville, TN

Dearest Jo,

Well Butch, how's your arm – I'm expecting an answer to this letter – a fast one at that, cause it sure seems a long time since you wrote last. I suppose you're wondering what goes on here – so I'll at least tell you what I know. To begin with we are about to start another phase of our training – It will not take place here. This is merely an examining station. They determine whether or not you're fit to go on. Anyway yours truly has passed half of the exam with success, that is the physical end. Took two days – it's one of the most rigid physicals I've ever taken. Most everything was checked by machines. They tell me the worst is yet to come, that is the psychological test – it will also take two days. If I fail that – well I'm just out. Lost a few of my best friends who washed out on the physical. Anyway it's a lot of fun while it lasts.

They have a weird setup down here – we get paid the full $105 instead of $75. But we have civilian cooks out here – so at the end of the month we pay them the $30 instead of the gov't. Of course the cooking is much better.

I'm sorry I couldn't write and tell you that I was leaving. But things happened so fast. I barely had time to scratch out a few lines to my people. If I pass this psychological I'll probably be sent to Maxwell or another one of the major air fields. If I don't -- ? Expect to be here at least two weeks.

How have you been Dear? How did your new job pan out? I've been rooting for you – hoping you'll make out alright.

I don't want to make any promises – but if I get a chance to get into Nashville I'll have a picture taken in my Cadet uniform – of course for you only.

> Love,
> Skip
> A.A.F.C.C. Sqd. F-2
> Nashville, Tennessee

P.S. You know I miss you Dear and it's been long since I've heard from you so don't delay.

Sept. 21, 1942
Nashville, TN

Dearest Jo,

Surprised dear!? Don't be. It may seem strange, me writing a letter a day. But you see we are restricted for 14 days. That leaves me seven nights a week to do nothing but think of you. It does me good to think of the past, but the future _____ it's all blank. Seriously, it ceases to be funny when I begin to wonder if I'll ever get the chance to see you again. From what I can gather all furloughs hereof are cancelled. Really hurts when you think it over a bit – Doesn't' it? For the present I must keep myself satisfied by looking at your picture. Believe me it helps! I suppose – to you – this doesn't sound true, coming from Skip. But give anyone here a beautiful night, soft music with nowhere to go – and if his thoughts don't back to the girl back home, well he just isn't human.

It is now 9 P.M. We're all listening to the radio – across from me sits a fellow who sang for Harry James in 1939. Why do I write about him? Well, he washed out on today's exam and is trying to figure out a way to break the news to his wife. I wonder what I would do if I was in his shoes – I dread even the thought of it. You know I give this outfit credit for one thing – took the stubbornness out of me, and that's something I had a lot of.

To tell you something about today's tests – seven hours of writing. Some of the subjects were math, aerial photography, physics and some on the mechanical side. All in one I found out how ignorant I am. Oh yes, I passed – but tomorrow is another day – some more exams on coordination and a few other things and believe me I had better do better than I did today. Anyway I know that you're rooting for me.

There has been a call for 950 pilots today – if my exams qualify me as such I'll be moving – soon. I've been thinking it must be pretty cold getting up in the morning back home – how do you manage?

Have you heard from any of the gang lately? I haven't had the time to write to anyone – but you. You know I don't mind you taking up my time. As a matter of fact I love it! Getting back to this place, regardless of what happens or what changes take place, it's wonderful to know there's someone back home who will never change. And I'm sure you won't disappoint me.

Love,
Skip

P.S. I'll try to remember and tell you that I love you somewhere in the letter thereby eliminating these P.S.'s. Just have enough time left to take one more good look at your picture before lights out. Good night Butch.

Love

Chapter 2 – 1942

Sept. 22, 1942
Nashville, TN

Dearest Jo,

I hate to complain dear, but if I don't receive any mail from you soon, I won't have anything to write about. On top of that I'll feel as though I am being neglected. You can see how much a person's environment has to do with his personal feelings. Can't go out as yet so I guess it's only natural that I should feel a little blue. I suppose the good in me, what little I have, emerges at times like this. But how about you dear? Surely these letters don't leave you feeling as though you have seen the last of me. You didn't, not if I can help it. Supposing it were so? I'd expect you to go around with a smile on your face identical to the one of the picture I have in front of me. Of course it's of you. No one else could have a smile as sweet as you. Need I remind you that I love you. If there is any truth to mental telepathy then you've been listening to me rave about you all week.

So Butch exams are completed, results – unknown. They certainly believe in keeping you in suspense around here. That doesn't mean that you have to do the same.

Love,
Skip

P.S. For financial reasons I'm sending these letters <u>Free</u> Mail. I'm beginning to wonder if they are reaching their destination. In case the others didn't – this is the third one this week.

Chapter 2 – 1942

Sept. 24, 1942
Nashville, TN

Dearest Jo,

Though it is highly impolite of me to remind you of a debt, do you realize that you now owe me four letters? It has been a big disappointment for me every day this week to find myself forgotten at each mail call, while all the other fellows sit around reading letters from those dearest to them. There I sit with nothing to cling to but a memory (of course it's a fond memory). Yet I know you are the only one capable of correcting this situation. (all this is off if I hear from you within the next twenty four hours). Then again the mail situation is just about hopeless around here unless my complete address is used, so be sure to write it just as I indicated in my first letter.

Your sister probably thinks I'm one _____ of a guy – not even a word about her in my letters. It isn't that I don't think of her – being pushed around all day leaves me just enough time to write to someone nearer me. (You, of course). How is her romance coming along? Did Vince get a furlough? If he did I know they had a wonderful time.

At the present everything is quiet around here. Maybe it's the calm before the storm. You know Butch the sooner I finish all of this – if I do, the sooner I can present you with that set of Silver Wings you love so much. Myself I like the silvery moon, but it just isn't complete without you. Speaking of songs how about "Take Me" – Bing is singing it now.

I would love to write to you tomorrow – but unless something happens – such as getting a letter from you I don't see how I can make it. Not getting any mail from you seems to be a good way of getting me to write, doesn't it? But don't overdo a good thing dear.

Love,
Skip

P.S. I have a funny feeling there's a letter on the way – and I'm almost certain I'll get it tomorrow.

Love Again
Skip

Oct. 4, 1942
Nashville, TN

Dearest Jo,

Well Darling, I have finally received your mail – three letters at once. You certainly had me wondering. Thoughts have been entering my mind a hundred a minute so that I did not know what to think You know what a relief it was to find out that everything is on the sunny side. Of course there is lots of room for improvement. Why can't I be fortunate enough to get one of those so called furloughs? Just to put my arms around you and have your lips brushing mine would be heavenly. Why only last night I lay dreaming of some of the wonderful evenings we have spent along – evenings that will never be equaled unless they are to be spent with only you. Recall an evening we lay nestled in each other's arms – with your tender body quivering against mine. Well Dear those were eves that one just can't take and brush off without a thought. At least I can't. It certainly does my heart good to know that there is a future – because I'm surely looking forward to seeing a lot of you.

Glad to hear about my best friend's good fortune. If he is still there when this letter reaches you tell him to take it easy a someday we may see each other. I know he'll have a damn good time or his name is not Zup. How many days did he get? Wouldn't surprise me one bit to see him and Fran get married –if they already hadn't. Give my best to Wimpy – but tell him to handle my doll with care.

Chapter 2 – 1942

Well Dear I must sign off as it is getting about that time – Dream Time – And I wouldn't disappoint my honey for the world. I remain always true to you – with loads of

Love,
Skip

P.S. Visited Nashville but it's so damn lousy there is nothing to write about. Just a one horse town full of the ignorant most unbecoming people I've ever had the pleasure of meeting.

Love Again
Skip

Oct. 11, 1942
Nashville, TN

Dearest Jo,

This will be a short letter as I haven't got time – you guessed it – moving again. Tonight I found out that I qualified as Bombardier Pilot. I'm moving tomorrow, where to? Looks as if all hopes of seeing you soon are shattered. I actually don't know how things will work out – regardless I'm sure everything will turn out for the better. I take it from your last letter that you're worrying too much – you know I wouldn't want you to do that even though it makes me feel good to know I'm still in your heart. Maybe I shouldn't write the type of letter to you that I have. They seem to leave you somewhat in the dark. As if you were sorry for things that had happened. Are you? As for me they'll be memories I'll forever cherish. Well "Darling I have to begin packing so _____ and be good.

Love
Skip

P.S. Save some of those good times for me as I do have some hopes of seeing you. I'll write as soon as I arrive.

Oct. 19, 1942
Nashville, TN (but postmarked on the road)

Dearest Jo,

Excuse all filth and dirt that will go along with this letter but under the conditions I just can't do better. It's my fourth day of travel and I'm pretty damn tired. It seems like I'll never reach my destination – California. Yes just what I was hoping for Santa Ana only about forty miles away from Zup. I sure hope I get the opportunity to see him. Anyway we expect to arrive sometime tomorrow. I'm fed up looking out of this window and not being able to see nothing but cactus plants. I'm going to throw this off at the next town – it may be Yuma Arizona. As you write later on let me know if you've received this little note.

Love
Skip

P.S. It's pretty damn tough writing on this train with it rocking back and forth but I suppose I can still write out that I love <u>you.</u>

Oct. 21, 1942
Santa Ana, CA

Dearest Jo,

I suppose you're just dying with anxiety to hear from me all about California including Los Angeles and Hollywood. Well dear I'd love to oblige – but I haven't seen a thing myself as yet. I will get this weekend off so I guess I'll take in Hollywood as it is only about thirty miles away from camp. I have had one awful let down up to date. For two hours I've been using the telephone and I couldn't get in touch with him no how. They told me from March Field that he moved to Fresno – at Fresno they tell me he was sent away but they won't tell me to where (military secret I suppose). I hope it's not over the pond. I'd certainly love to see him again. If he were here you can imagine what a beating Hollywood would have taken (including Lana Turner). Maybe it was fate – who knows? I didn't give up yet though. I still think I'll see him. Have you heard anything? Try and get his new address dear – please?

As for myself they are running me pretty ragged – on the go most of the day signing papers and more papers – the same old story never a dull moment. I understand this is a nine week course so I'll be here quite some time – long enough to get around a little. Perhaps you have heard the news today. We had an earthquake, didn't do no damage, knocked all the clothes off the hangars though. They'll have to dispense with that stuff as I'm allergic to noise. Did you get my letter from Yuma? If it stays cloudy all day there you can go anywhere and get a free meal. The trip all in one was okay outside of being tiring as all hell. We traveled the Shore Route. In short we went down through Tennessee into Alabama, Mississippi (I'm down on my spelling, it's been a long time since grade school) Louisiana, Texas, New Mexico, Arizona and into California. I'd love to make that trip with you some day. You could hear someone talk about it all day but you really wouldn't enjoy it till you actually saw everything (seeing is believing). How about yourself Dear? It's been sometime since I heard from you. I'm certain you won't delay in answering. When will I get to see you again? Do you have any idea? As for myself I'll keep quiet cause it seems everything I wish for never turns out right.

I'll just have to fill this sheet up as it is a long time between letters. This sheet I reserved for you only! What I wouldn't give to have you in my arms this minute. I feel ashamed of myself now letting those precious moments go to waste when I could have spent them with you. Live and learn. I believe I've learned my lesson. You were sweet though taking everything pretty well. Do you miss me Dear? Or do I deserve to be missed? Heaven knows if I ever get you in my arms again you'll cry for mercy. I have a confession to make. My last night in Nashville I got a little tipsy and one of my friends had a tattoo put on my arm. Now I'm trying to find out how to get the damn thing off. Well Dear I'm going to expect a letter from you at least every other day. (that's an order). If not you had better have a good excuse. Naturally I'm going to do my best to keep your mailman pretty busy. Signing off with loads of love, hugs and kisses.

> Love
> Skip
> Sqd 83 Bomb. Wing
> S.A.A.A.B.
> Santa Ana, Calif

P.S. I'll bet Vince and Helen had a wonderful time. Tell her I'm sorry I couldn't give her no competition for the sofa.

Oct. 22, 1942
Santa Ana, CA

Dearest Jo,

Well hon, here's that pesty boyfriend of yours again. So far away and yet so close. After all we're no worse off than we were before. Except for the fact that it may take our letters a few days more to reach their destination. I'm sure we'll remedy that by writing more often. (As you can see I've already started.) Whether I finish this letter tonight or not is hard to say. Everyone in the barracks is doing something – polishing shoes, arranging footlockers – preparing for tomorrow morning's inspection and if I intend to go out this weekend I better get eager myself. Everything is beginning to shape into something out here – including the hazing from the new upper classmen. Let's leave the service for awhile and go back to civilization. What do the young ladies back home think of their dashing hero Errol Flynn? Or have you heard. I'm expecting to hear a lot from you, it's been sometime since you've written so your arms should be rested up by now. Were you surprised to find out that I've been sent to California? I should have a lot to talk about after all this is over – that is if I live through it. Naturally I have hopes – I can't bear to think of fading away just yet – I haven't seen enough of you yet. I figured it out and this course will be finished by Christmas so I've got my fingers crossed. Back to the service – I was forced to get another haircut but it's not half as bad as the first one I had. The fellows with me, here have no previous military experience, other than cadet training, right now they are wondering how I'll have everything ready for tomorrow morning. I'll teach them the ropes later. But I forgot to ask you. Do you still love me dear? Or do I have to ask? You know if someone else should step in, well you know Skip if you gave it to me straight without beating around the bush I'd probably laugh it off and forget it. What made me think of that anyway? Maybe it's a hunch. Remember Dear all I permit you to do is hold hands. Save the rest of your loving for me. I think I can take care of it don't you. I wonder sometime how everything will turn out. It certainly is a problem for Doctor Anthony _____ remember? Well Butch if I keep this up I won't have much left for next time and I do want the mail to you to be getting there at regular intervals. I just read an article in the paper which stated that Hedy Lamar was freelancing – I'll have to give her a tumble. Of course my love for her will have to ration – That's something you'll never have to worry about.

Love
Skip

P.S. With your picture up on the shelf for inspection I know I won't have a thing to worry about. Remember I'm expecting an immediate answer. Goodnight Dear and pleasant dreams.

(One of these mornings you may awake and find me beside you. How would you like that?)

Love
Skip

Chapter 2 – 1942

Oct. 25, 1942
Sunday Noon
Santa Ana, CA

Dearest Jo,

Back in camp again after a wonderful day in Santa Ana It's a beautiful place without a doubt. People are very sociable – at least they know there is a war going on. The night clubs are swell – wonderful entertainment. The only drawback – a cadet cannot buy a drink after 10:00 P.M. to save his soul. The trolleys are something that struck me as being funny – they are so huge and awkward – they're just not becoming to the town in the least. If Santa Ana is supposed to be just a sample of what L.A. looks like, well I know I'm going to like it here. The girls around here certainly go in for wearing pants – and sweaters. Right outside the post is a country club. A big golf tournament is going to start at 2:00 P.M. 48 prominent stars are to be there including Bing Crosby so you know I can't miss that. There's so damn many places to go – you just don't know where to start. I only hope I have the time and money to see half of what I have in mind of seeing.

When I stop to think awhile I wonder if all this is really happening to me. I must admit I've got some wonderful breaks in this man's army. If it weren't for this war the odds are that I would have never seen California. What we couldn't do out here together! I know it's an impossibility but it makes a wonderful dream. How would you like to spend the winter down here? I'll see what I can do for you. Why don't you try enlisting in the WAAC's. That might get you down here. (If you do I'll break your neck). The little snapshot is me so don't let it frighten you. Do you think I've changed. I lost weight only 150 now – I can't understand it – you must have something to do with that. The results of love must be showing on me. But I love it. Well hon it's about 1:00 P.M. and I have to start getting dressed for this golf tournament so I'll have to cut this letter short. I'm hoping you're not taking things too hard. Take my advice, relax and go out and enjoy yourself. It does the body and soul both good. And then again there is a future so that we will be able to make up for lost time – if you don't change your mind by then. My favorite song – I'm Dreaming of a White Christmas (only I don't know if it will be white). Be good.

Love
Skip

P.S. I'll bet you spend all day Sunday sleeping.

Oct. 26, 1942, 27, 28
Santa Ana, CA

Dearest Jo,

After reading this letter, I don't want you to feel as though I'm welching on a promise I made in one of my first letters – to write at least every other day. Also I don't want you to feel as though I'm crying on your shoulder when I give you my reason for not being able to hold to my promise. I'm beginning this letter Monday night but heaven knows when I'll finish as for the next three weeks I'll have about fifteen minutes every evening to myself. The schedule is really rugged. Absolutely no time off outside of Sunday. Only seventeen books to study out of – calisthenics – drill – and from seven to 9:30 every evening a compulsory study hall. Lights must be out at 10:00 every evening. – (Oh for the life of a cadet).

I had a nice time Sunday afternoon – but I didn't get quite as big a kick out of it as I thought I would. When you see so many prominent actors together they don't look different from anyone else. There goes the bugle for lights out – Goodnight.

So another day has rolled around. Not quite as bad as yesterday though. Spent the afternoon shooting the Thompson submachine gun – the best part of this whole thing was that we got in about three hours swimming in the ocean – If you really want to get a kick out of swimming you ought to try it some time – it's a wonderful feeling

Chapter 2 – 1942

swimming away out and out of no where a big wave comes along and almost tosses you ashore. Can you imagine swimming in the latter part of October? This life has some good points at that.

I received your letter today dear. It was postmarked the twenty fifth so it only takes two days time for your mail to get here – at that rate I should receive about three letters a week. Getting back to your letter it was nice of you to mail me Zup's address although I doubt if I'll have time to write to him. However you've got me wondering as to what was in the letter that was returned to you. You should have never torn it up. Could it be possible for you to write it over again? Does my heart good to know that you care for me. As for me being a bombardier pilot – I'm not one as yet – although I've got all the necessary qualifications to become one – if everything goes right it will take at least four more months. So you see it takes a lot of damn work and patience to get anything out of this man's army. What gripes me is you go through all the studying – make one trip over and may never get back.

This is Wednesday afternoon – third day I'm writing this letter. It happens to be raining today so we can't go out for calisthenics. Of course they have something to do in case of rain. Today for instance we are to clean up the barracks now – that makes it pretty easy for me to goof off. That's about all that goes on around here except that I have to take my tetanus shots all over – also have to go through the pressure chamber equivalent to about 30,000 ft.

I think Zup has a pretty good idea of his dad's condition – in one of his letters he told me about the doctors not being able to do nothing for him. It sure is tough but the way things stand at the present I don't imagine not one of our lives is worth much. So I still think I was right in saying there is never a tomorrow so enjoy yourself while you can. If I sound a little off the beam forgive me dear but a million and one things are hitting me back of the head at once – so that's probably just the way I'm writing. You sure don't have much to say as to your activities back home. Don't you go out nowhere? Or do anything?

Chapter 2 – 1942

This time I'll stop writing for good till I start the next letter – which will be tomorrow no doubt.

                    Love
                    Skip

P.S. The book of etiquette says it's improper to write postscripts as they are written in a hurry – usually and therefore you may write something you would be sorry for later. On the contrary I'm certain I am not sorry for all I want to say is I Love You. You know under the conditions this letter was written so I'm sure you'll excuse all the errors & erasures.

                    Love
                    Skip

Oct. 30, 1942
Santa Ana, CA

Dearest Jo,

We finally succeeded in getting some time off even though it took an epidemic to do it. Two fellows in my Sqd. contracted scarlet fever somewhere – of course that means quarantine. We got some good news today. We'll get a going over by the doctor tomorrow and if no one else has it we get the weekend off. About your letters dear, I have a complaint to make – received one today and so help me they're getting shorter. So you had better get on the ball and start filling them pages up.

How about this Mike – who is he? My rival? From all indications he must be interested as to what my intentions are toward you – Am I right? Of course there are certain things you are withholding from me. I suppose that's why I can't treat the situation accordingly. To my estimation if I once broke an engagement I wouldn't care to see the

Chapter 2 – 1942

girl again. At times love is one hell of a subject to discuss – isn't it? Of all the smart men (and women) we have in this country it seems that someone should have found an appropriate definition but up to the present all we have had was some good guesses. May I offer my explanation? It's very short but to the point – It's something I have for you call it what you want. – yearning, likeness, admiration – I believe are all components of the word love. Now I'm getting too technical I should be telling you of my love for you instead of trying to act the part of a professor.

One thing I want to remind you of and I am serious – Don't for the love of Pete go around bragging too damn much about how good I'm doing. True up to the present everything is coming along fine but all it takes is one little slip and you're done – with no excuses accepted. (One of the main cadet rules are – no excuses.) If and when I do finish this successfully, I'll go back home and brag a little myself (I think it's something to brag about). Looking at it the other way – if I should wash out I'd probably dig myself a hole and forget about the rest of the world.

As I have stated previously we don't get too much time to ourselves – whenever we do though I devote most of it to you. That is wondering what you're doing or else what we would be doing were I home. We did spend some wonderful moments together. Times when no one in the world seemed to exist but the two of us remember? Maybe I'm getting too mushy now – am I? You have never commented on my writing such letters so you leave me wondering.

It's not like me to withhold anything from you. I'll tell you what a surprise I've got today. Do you remember when Vince and I left for camp together. Do you recall him telling you about the girls we met on the train. Well I received a letter from one of these girls and she's trying to convince me that there is such a thing as love at first sight. It's been so long that I actually didn't expect to hear from her. In my spare time I'll write her a letter that will make her hair stand on edge.

Chapter 2 – 1942

Speaking of movies – I believe seeing the actors in person spoil the enjoyment you would get out of the movie otherwise. And as for your sister being chicken hearted – how about yourself? You're not hard hearted yourself – I should know. If you are you've kept it pretty well hidden from me.

I will not accept no excuses from you for a short letter –if I can write three pages (very small writing at that) you should be able to fill up anywhere around twelve pages easily. After all it's supposed to be a sugar report. It is now 9 P.M. that leaves me an hr. to brush up on my physics. It's got me stumped somewhat. Now that Olga's boyfriend is in the army you two should get along pretty well at work anyway – plenty to talk about, that helps pass the time away.

Love
Skip

P.S. Don't worry about me pulling an Errol Flynn with all these women around everywhere you have to watch they don't do
_____. I'll bet the civilians have a picnic around here – no army camps nothing to hinder them as far as women are concerned. I feel for you getting up these cold winter morning. But think of me and it may warm you up a little. My my I'm beginning to think a lot of myself again so I'll sign off before I get too rugged.

Love
Skip

Oct. 31, 1942
Santa Ana, CA

Dearest Jo,

I suppose you are wondering as to what kind of a weekend I have spent. Well here it is right in the barracks twiddling my thumbs. Isn't that a wonderful thing to be doing on a Halloween night? Apparently

Chapter 2 – 1942

the hospital staff is somewhat worried about this scarlet fever epidemic – must be more serious than I have anticipated. That of course means we are quarantined to the barracks area. Not even permitted to attend church services. This evening they have strung up sheets in between our beds as an added precaution. What burned me up mostly they had to wait till we got dressed ready to go before telling us this. This gives me all day Sunday to catch up on my mail. If I write anymore to you – I'll be forced to tell you what goes on by the hour instead of by the day like I've been doing (I know you'd love that.)

I must tell you of my experience in the low pressure chamber today. They took us up to 20,000 ft. without giving us the oxygen masks. I got the funniest sensation – fingers began to tingle at the tips – got cold as hell. While at that height they gave us all some simple arithmetic problems and you should have seen some of the foolish answers. Mine was to subtract two from a hundred, my answer was 97 and so help me I thought I was putting down the correct answer. It all goes to show you that at that height your mind and body does not function properly without the employment of oxygen. After that we put on the masks and went up to 30,000 – it didn't bother no one in the least – just slowed up the heart beat. Coming down was toughest. The pressure builds up so great against your eardrums and you think your head is busting. When we dropped down to 15,000 two of the boys passed out like a light – so we had to level off till they came too – then come down slowly. (Would you like to try it.)

Your letters are so short Dear – you just don't give me much to write about. What would you do if you were to write me a letter a day? (I'll bet you couldn't do it), You won't make me angry trying.

This damn war situation is nothing to sneeze at – looks like we lost another airplane carrier today. If we don't damn soon start shelling out some action ourselves I hate to think of the outcome. I'm for getting it over in a hurry one way or another. I'm tired of being fattened up for the kill.

Chapter 2 – 1942

So you liked the picture – thank you. You know it's pretty hard to make arrangements to take a big photo – you can't get it taken on the post and when you go out you've got so much to do you just don't worry about trifles. If I don't get some taken damn soon I'm afraid my own mother will stop writing.

Well I hope no one plays no Halloween pranks on you. I'm forced to sign off as I have a headache – you can tell by the way the lines in the letter are running. I still feel like I'm up about 30,000 ft. yet.

Love
Skip

Nov. 6, 1942
Santa Ana, CA

Dearest Jo,

Always surprising me – I must admit. It was sweet of you Jo but I wish you wouldn't. You must understand that it is quite a distance between the East and West coast – so that by the time a package does arrive here it certainly takes its share of knocks. Besides I've written to you of the food out here – it's second best to none. So please don't go pulling any more such surprises on me. I don't intend for you to think that I don't appreciate what you've done or the trouble you've gone through but under the circumstances Jo, it is really best if you don't.

From the doctors final diagnosis I find that it won't be long before this damn quarantine is lifted. (Thank God) What a relief that will be! I can just imagine myself going out now and letting off some of this steam which has accumulated during the past few days. I know it won't be necessary to pull an (Errol Flynn) as the girls around here are very weak when it comes to resistance.

Chapter 2 – 1942

Boys will be boys – even with all this work on their hands – they are continuously fooling around. I'm writing you a little ditty made up by the gang during study period – but first I want you to believe me when I say I didn't have nothing to do with it – I'm not that bright. (Don't let the beginning frighten you. It's really not as bad as it sounds.

I remember the first time I tried it
I was only a kid of fifteen
And even tho' she was much younger than me
She was much more composed and serene

I was eager – yet awkwardly backward,
Uncertain of how to proceed
But she seemed not to notice the hesitance
With which I prepared for the deed

I was out in the barn I remember
At the close of a lush summer day
The evening was scented with clover in bloom
And the fragrance of freshly mowed hay

I remember I spoke to her softly
As I cuddled her face in my hands
As I saw in the depths of her wise eyes the look
Of a loved one who understands

I remember she moved a bit closer
And the touch of her body was warm
As my fingers moved awkwardly over her throat
While she nestled her head in my arms

Long after I stood up uncertain
Of whether to stay or run
A tingle with pride – yet shaken and awed
As I knew that at last it was done

Chapter 2 – 1942

I remember (it seemed hours later)
How my heart hammered under my blouse
With the pride of a boy who turned into a man
As I made my way back to the house

Twenty years have gone by since that evening
But I've never forgotten I vow
The thrill and joy I felt as a boy
On the day when I first milked a cow.

By the Fighting 83rd

Well it may not have been so good as that – but it served its purpose –
helped fill in the empty space.

Love
Skip

Nov. 8, 1942
Santa Ana, CA

Dearest Jo,

Time, time – it's something that is certainly rationed. It's what I'm
fighting against now. On to that add the lack of sleep and I assure you
it's some predicament to be in while trying to write a letter. If it was
to anyone but you, I wouldn't give the idea another thought. I know it
would be impossible to sleep without having a nightmare if I wouldn't
at least try to live up to my end of the agreement. At the time I
suggested it I didn't quite realize what a tremendous task it would
turn out to be (I love it.)

I covered a good bit of ground this weekend – started out in Balboa
from there I went to Los Angeles and ended up in Hollywood at the
Stage Door Canteen. Every minute of my time was well taken care of.
I got the biggest kick out of dancing with Dinah Shore and not

knowing who she was till the dance was over. All through the dance I had been feeding her a helluva line – working on the old flattery angle, of course – Imagine my embarrassment upon finding out her identity. She was one good sport though, joked around and had a few drinks with me. The place is loaded with celebrities and they get as much kick out of everything as we do.

So your brother is thinking of getting married – well why not. If to his way of reasoning he thinks he's right well there isn't the slightest doubt that he is right. It's just the other way around with me though – if I were only engaged to you, let alone being married, I wouldn't feel right about going out the way I am. The way things are now I don't have a guilty conscience and I know I'm not depriving you of anything. But there I go ravin on and on. I could probably do that for weeks on the subject of marriage – It's too bad I haven't got the time. Well I'll whisper more to you – when I get to see you. Soooooo, I must say good night, my eyes just refuse to stay open.

Love
Skip

Nov. 12, 1942
Santa Ana, CA

Dearest Jo,

Now that the old burg has been honored with another visit by one of its former men about town I'll bet the activity has been brought back up to par. But I don't begrudge him in the least. After all I did have more than my share of furlough time. It appears that the old boy has really been stung by the love bug, doesn't it? I don't agree with him on the idea of getting married while in the service. They say love has no barriers – hooey! If I were your husband and came back minus a couple of arms how would you feel? If you say you still love me – hooey again, it would be nothing but sheer sympathy. So kindly inform him that if he has any silly ideas in his head he'd better forget them – besides I can't be there to be his best man! I haven't got time to write him but I wish you'd tell him to take a stroll around the block between sixth and fifth street – he'll understand. I wouldn't pass my opinion on anyone but Zup – coming from me I know how he would take it.

I take it from your letter that you're in a belligerent mood – angry at the world. You feel like everyone is getting the breaks but you. You're wrong the same thing goes on here – all you hear is bitch and more bitching all day long – I do it myself, that's why I know it's wrong. Some day I'll write to my congressman to see what I can do about getting an army camp set up around home – just to give you girls a break. You'll fall in love every day and forget even faster – never a dull moment.

The barracks has taken on a homey appearance – each man was issued an arm chair. It serves its purpose as well as a shirt and pant hanger at night.

I'm now a full pledged member of the Goldbrickers association – sprained my ankle the other day playing soccer, so I got a five day excuse from calisthenics that gives me an hour and a half to write letters in.

Well I've written about everything from peanuts to crackerjack and outside of saying I still love you I want to thank you for the wonderful job you're doing writing letters.

Love
Skip

This blank space hurts me but I can't help it.

Chapter 2 – 1942

Friday 13th
Santa Ana, CA

Dearest Jo,

Whatever gave you the idea that I didn't care to write to you? If I didn't – you know I just wouldn't. My attitude toward letter writing has changed considerably from the time I joined the air force. It appears to be a wonderful form of relaxation – something I can use a lot of.

Can't you girls find something more exciting to do than go to Bill's or the Falcon Hall for an evening of fun. Small wonder though, since most of the men are away. As for you and I hitting that potent stuff – that's definitely out. I think I've abused myself enough – there may be a future.

It's a shame that not even one of your brothers can be home for the holidays – I know it will be a miserable day on both ends. Of course you know it's impossible for me to be there – that's why I hate to even talk about it.

One thing I want to remind you of – for heaven's sake don't go around spending your money foolishly – I know you work for it and it's no picnic. Besides I've got all I need – that is everything but you! Incidentally if you can wrap yourself up and air mail yourself down here – well I can dream, can't I?

Again I want to thank you for the wonderful way in which you are handling our correspondence. You know it make me feel damn good to receive a letter at least every other day. When I get a little more free time, I won't let you down.

Love
Skip

Chapter 2 – 1942

Monday Nite
Santa Ana, CA

Dearest Jo,

Before I begin to write this letter – I warn you, one of those moods have hit me again. Anymore they appear to be coming along at regular intervals and I feel as though writing to you about it will remedy any pain or sorrow that I have. The one reason I despise writing such a letter is the effect it will probably have on you. To think for a moment that it would cause you to lose that beautiful smile of yours – would take the bottom out of my heart. At a time like this all those beautiful squabbles we've had come back to me. No doubt they were an omen of true love. And honestly Butch, I smile to myself when I think of those silly little lies I used to tell you – but they were white lies. Why only last night I dreamt of those wonderful evenings we spent together – of the silly but enchanting things we talked about, I'd give anything to go through it all again.

So it's with a kiss upon your tender lips and with these thoughts in my mind that I'll eventually wander off into the land of dreams. It frightens me to think that I may never get to see my loved ones again. Assuming that I am an average fellow, with memories such as this it's no small wonder that the common soldier goes to battle with a spirit that can't be beat. As the time for lights is limited I was forced to give you only a condensation of what I really wanted to write about. So here's that kiss dear.

Love
Skip

P.S. I hope this doesn't fill my peep-eye with tears – as I know she has enough to worry about and think about, without me adding to the burden she is already so bravely shouldering.

Keep Em Smiling
Skip

Chapter 2 – 1942

Thursday Eve (postmarked Nov. 27, 1942)
Santa Ana, CA

Dearest Jo,

It's Thanksgiving – but just another day as far as the army is concerned. Oh! They tried their best to make everyone feel as though they were at home, at the dinner table. The food with all the trimmings was there – but that certain something that it really takes to make one realize it is Thanksgiving, was missing. Well I'm thankful to be alive, and consider myself very fortunate to have the love of the sweetest girl on earth. And it hurts me to know that I can't return my love otherwise than by mail.

Well Darling, I had a feeling you would get a better position and I'm very glad indeed to learn that it was in the Westinghouse. I know it means making a few sacrifices such as not being able to see your friends, but it's well worth it. If anyone deserves the breaks, you do.

I received your letter today, and perhaps without you realizing it – it was well timed. It appears as though it takes more time for delivery than it did before. You didn't have much to say about your job, Why? You know I'm just dying with curiosity to hear all about how you're doing.

I only hope this letter will be as well timed as yours and reaches you for the weekend. I would write more but that old Holiday spirit got the best of me, causing me to write something I shouldn't. Then you'd refuse to write – I don't want that to happen. So with loads of love and lots of luck in your new job I remain yours forever with

Love
Skip

Chapter 2 – 1942

Dec. 6, 1942
Santa Ana, CA

Dearest Jo,

Making excuses for not writing appears to be a habit with me – but some excuse is better than none at all. To be truthful I've had my hands full this past week, Christmas shopping and final exams in two major subjects – math and physics – I still don't know if I passed them or not – next week I'll get the news.

However I do have some good news in the making – they are supposed to open up an advanced training center for us in Aberdeen, Md. Imagine only 300 miles from home. Things look bright as we are the next class to graduate.

I'm glad to hear you're coming along fine in your work. But don't go breaking your back – it's not worth it.

I have to cut this short if I don't I'll get too damn sentimental and this is no time for it. I certainly hope your Christmas will be more merry than mine. But remember I love you. And about the best gift you could send me – would be your love.

Love
Skip

Dec. 8, 1942
Santa Ana, CA

Dearest Jo,

The last letter was rather short so I'm following it up with a few more lines. To begin with I'm not feeling very well – contracted a damn sore throat somewhere and it appears to be giving me a little trouble.

Chapter 2 – 1942

Received your gift today honey – what can I say but thanks a million. Were I home, undoubtedly I would express my gratitude differently.

This set of wings caught my eye in the PX and I just remembered you haven't any air force insignia. Well these aren't as good as they could be but right now there isn't much to choose from. I only hope they get there without falling out as I haven't the opportunity to pack them.

Are you getting much time off for the holidays, more than I am, I hope. A little thought for you to cherish just before I sign off – regardless who you're with on Christmas Eve, you know my heart will be there also – thumping away that monotonous but sweet old phrase, I love you.

Love
Skip

Dec. 14, 1942
Santa Ana, CA

Dearest Jo,

For once I have what you might call an iron clad alibi or a damn good excuse for not writing. I was just released from the hospital this morning – had a bad case of tonsillitis with a temperature of 102.5. Anyway it was enough to keep me in that damn hell hole five days. Remember, I did complain about my throat in a previous letter – it finally worked out on me. I feel good now that the fever is down. Five whole days without writing to anyone (didn't want to worry you) and still not much to write about. We are supposed to have our Xmas party sometime this weekend. I suppose everyone will have a good time as they will have all they want to eat and drink. The girls are also included in the deal. As yet I'm in doubt whether I'll go or not. I don't see how I can possibly have a good time without you. What have you got planned for the holidays, dear? Whatever it may be I know I'm missing a damn good time.

So Darling once more I can feel my temperature rising – but I know that it is just my blood tingling over the mere thought of you. It is with this wonderful feeling running through me that I'll leave you for the present.

Love
Skip

Dec, 1942
Santa Ana, CA

Christmas card

A Christmas message for my Sweetheart

I love each thing about you.
Your voice, Dear; and your smile,
The pleasant things you say and do
To make Life so worthwhile;
But the best of all the reasons
Why I love you as I do,
Can be stated very simply..
It is just because YOU'RE YOU!

F.O. Spencer (Pilot), F.O. Richards (Co-Pilot),
Lt. Skibinski (Bomb-Nav), Sgt. Jones (Eng-Gunner),
Sgt. Paskin (Radio-Gunner), and Sgt. Watson (Armorer)

Chapter 3
1943

Chapter 3 – 1943

Jan. 4, 1943
Santa Ana, CA

Dearest Jo,

I know I've been rather lax in answering your mail and I beg your forgiveness for not being more prompt. I felt so terrible all through the holidays that I just couldn't bring myself into a writing mood. Oh Yes! I've tried but it was to no avail – the more I tried the heavier got my heart – bringing on that hollow feeling deep down inside. Anyway on to a little news about myself. Yours truly has completed this course with flying colors. As a reward (if you want to call it that) they made me a Cadet Lt. and transferred me into Sqd 93 to help train a group of new recruits – that means no weekends off. I expect to be moved into advanced in a few weeks, but I'm beginning to wonder if it's worth it. The class before us graduated from advanced last Sunday. They got their wings and commission in one hand plus overseas tickets in the other. God! I don't know if I can bear that. Imagine not being able to see your loved ones before going over? Only now am I beginning to realize what a weakling I really am and I'm not in the least bit ashamed to admit it!! Oh it's not going over and perhaps getting blown out of the sky that worries me – It's the thought of not being able to see you again that's driving me whacky. And you ask me if I miss you – If you only realized how much!! Why I'd give anything just to hold you in my arms once more – To hear you say you still love me – I assure you – you wouldn't have to fight to kiss me. I'm sorry about for all those kisses I didn't take when I was in a position to do so. This letter will undoubtedly make you blue but Darling I want to always picture you smiling even if worse comes to worse. Give my best to all the rest, my love alone keep for your own.

Love
Skip

P.S. I want you to keep the fact that I probably won't get leave under your hat. Hate like hell to worry Mom you know.

Chapter 3 – 1943

Jan. 6, 1943
Santa Ana, CA

Dearest Jo,

The last thing I'd do in this world is disappoint you. If I have Darling, it was purely unintentional or else it couldn't be helped. You see – I have one helluva job now – makes me feel like a G.I. Chaplain when the weekend rolls around. I've got sixty men who want out and I'm forced to keep two thirds of them in for details. You can imagine the stories I'm forced to listen to. I wished that you would have a swell time over the holidays – but if you felt anywhere near the way I did, I know my wish didn't come true. Butch, you hurt me, telling me I don't care to write to you – and then you say that's a good reason for not writing me. Before I go Darling, I must ask you, Do you love me? If you do, you ought to write so much more. If you don't, well let's not even think of that. I did say that the holidays were something terrible. To be frank with you I didn't do a thing socially. I did thank the Good Lord for taking good care of you and I through the past year and asked that He guide you through the new one. I am thankful for having the sweetest girl on earth for my own. Before I wonder off here's a little ditty that tells the way I feel about you:

Your letters help to ease the hours.
They're filled with endearing charms
But your letters aren't quite enough
For, Darling, they haven't arms.

Love
Skip

Chapter 3 – 1943

January 11, 1943
Santa Ana, CA

Darling,

There is such a word in the English language which covers fully the way I feel on this, your birthday – it is humility. Most boyfriends, no matter what the barrier of distance, would have sent a cascade of flowers or such a similar expression of their love – but I didn't. There are oh so many ways in which I could lie myself back into your good graces. Still all I can say is a simple "I love you, Darling" and hold my breath until you say that you understand. Believe me, dear, at this moment I feel as though someone has driven a spike through my heart because I was so thoughtless – and my heart refuses to beat further until you tell me everything is alright, But I want you to know that even if I didn't send a token of my love and adoration for you, you have always been and always will be in my heart – and no matter how negligent I might seem from time to time, I want you to know that I will love so long as I am able to draw a breath.

As I sit here brooding in the not too quiet atmosphere of the barracks your picture keeps staring accusingly down at me from above the shelf. And for some powerful whimsy of fate – tonight your picture has taken on tremendous animation. Right now as I look again out of fearful eyes – you seem to be scowling at me, but somehow I can't help notice a tiny smile light the blueness of your eyes.

I am not a model boyfriend, Butch, and I don't pretend to be. But I challenge without fear that no one ever loved a woman more than I love you. Perhaps I could have said this more in the past – for I know now so desperately that I want nothing more than to go through life saying it over and over again to you.

There isn't much more I can say – I could use us reams of paper to excuse myself, but I know only too well what I've done. So, my

Chapter 3 – 1943

Darling, if ever a man needed forgiveness it is me. And all I want from you is a letter saying that everything is alright.

I close

Forever Yours
Skip

January 24, 1943
Roswell, New Mexico

Dearest,

I haven't heard from you for quite some time now – but it's undoubtedly due to the fact that I'm moving so much. Yes, I've moved again into a place that's indescribable – it's truly God's country – Roswell, New Mexico. Supposedly the second largest city in the state – it takes approximately five minutes to travel the length of the town. As for the field it's pretty nice – not a pursuit ship on the line – all twin engine bombers, namely, AT 11's, AT 17's and B-25's. Personally I'm hoping to do my flying in a B-25, it's much safer.

If everything goes right, in the next twelve weeks I'll receive my wings and commission. Then I'm going to be in there fighting for that long awaited furlough. Darling I wonder if you truly know how much I miss you. Only when I get to hold you in my arms again will you fully realize how much you mean to me. I lie awake at night thinking you're here beside me – hearing your voice so truthfully saying that you love me. Oh! I must have been an awful heel to sit there and act as if it didn't mean a thing to me. Honestly dear, those were the very words I wanted you to say over and over again. How I regret all that now and believe me Darling I won't have a moment's rest until I make amends for all the wrong I've ever did you. You know I'm longing to hear from you, so please don't keep me waiting.

Love
Skip

P.S Have just been issued all fur-lined high altitude flying equipment. What a sight I look – you should see me. Yes, yes, there is still enough space to say I love you.

January 28, 1943
Roswell Army Flying School
Roswell, New Mexico

Dearest,

Brrr! I feel right at home – reason – at least I've seen snow, and believe me it looks good. It wasn't much but it was the same white crystal like stuff I've seen back in good old Pa. The wind blows something terrific out here. In all the weather was so bad yesterday that all airplanes were grounded.

As much as I'd like to tell you what I do around here – I can't. I'm under oath and therefore not at liberty to discuss or write about my affairs (military of course) with no one. So when you do write, I wish you wouldn't inquire about them.

Now that leaves me even less to write about. So from here on I'll have to write about you. Well I'll begin with the bad points! To begin with you are very stubborn (but I love it). Sometimes I wonder how we two can ever get along. I'm on the stubborn side myself, you know. Secondly you chew on your fingernails – which is very very bad. (Something I don't have time to do.) Then again there are times when you try to act silly – believe me you really are silly then – very, very unbecoming to you. (I think all that ought to bring me a good long letter informing me that I'm no angel.)

But there must be some good wherever there is bad so let's get on with your good points. Your Heart – only a very small portion of it is enough to make up for your faults. To discuss it thoroughly would take days so to shorten it I'll just say it's made of gold. You are true in your promises, determined and very forgiving (Thank God) and your smile – well the moment I saw it, you had me hooked. Seriously Darling – I miss everything about you good or bad – and it can't be soon till I get to see you.

The WAAC's are moving on this field March 1st. That will be the extent of our social life. Then when we are bad boys I suppose they will give us a (WAAC) and send us to bed.

Well Darling by the time you receive this I'll have about eleven more weeks to go. Can't wait till I get to see you. Oh well, Praise the Lord and pass me my commission.

Love
Skip

P.S. I love you Darling.

Feb. 2, 1943
Roswell, New Mexico

My Dear Shakespeare:

I can't possibly begin to tell you how pleased and delighted I am to know you are still thinking of me. Of course, what does it matter to my antediluvian brain whether or not you write me? And the mere fact that I haven't heard from you in two weeks shouldn't trouble you one iota. Pray tell, have you broken a tibia or a femur, or something? Or perhaps your sacroiliac kiltered out of joint? Or maybe your digits need a massage? I really believe you have come to great physical harm, for what else could have happened?

Chapter 3 – 1943

Now, were I so coarse as to have forgotten to write you naturally I would shy away from even hinting that you were somewhat, shall I say "neglectful" However, as I point out the fact, irrelative as it may seem, that I have written you – not once but twice! I am not asking for a Congressional Medal of Honor, however I believe you need some sort of material inducement in order to provoke some mail from you. Need I say more?

Love
Skip

Tuesday (Morn) (postmarked Feb 9, 1943)
Roswell, New Mexico

Dearest,

It's 2 A.M. and I just finished reading your letter. It's just the type of letter I love to get from you. I haven't got the time to write and tell you everything as I must get a few hours sleep. I believe this will be the toughest week here. Ground School to Noon from Noon till Supper Flying, from Supper till 1 or 2 A.M. something. Believe it or not I didn't have time to shave today. What I'm trying to do is prove to you that I may not be able to write any more this week. All the more reason you should write. I wonder if you could send me a fifteen page letter? Take a chance. I know you could if you tried hard enough. There really is a lot to write about – you and I – that's enough, isn't it?

I can't help but remark a little on that one paragraph of yours – about us not realizing things, till it was too late. So help me I'm not sorry for anything that we've went through. Only at times temptation was so great – that up to this day I controlled myself as much as I did (wasn't much was it?). But at time like that a man is like a beast his desires must be fulfilled or else he goes whacky. I'm curious as to what it will be like when I get to see you – Sure I make promises to myself to be a little angel – but one look at you and they are all forgotten.

As for our children – 3 is a large order. We slept together a few nights and nothing happened. Perhaps I haven't got the finesse or technique call it what you want. If there was any truth to mental telepathy – I would have been in your arms quite a lot this past week. You'll be in mine this morning.

Love
Skip

P.S. I'm sorry for that last letter Darling. Forgiven?

(Postmarked Feb. 7, 1943)
Roswell, New Mexico

Dearest Jo,

I'm calling Falcon Hall at present. It may be a trifle late. I hope it's not as you may be there. That's the one thing that gets in my hair – at times I'd just love to call you and no phone – I'm beginning to wonder if anyone is up at the Falcon Hall at this time. I did tell you I'm sorry for that last, rather crude epistle I wrote. But I'm sure you understand. If I didn't love you would I dare write such a letter? Remember, I love you Darling. I'm hoping you're at the Hall so I can hear your voice once again.

Love
Skip

P.S. I/ we call him Billy we will have to name her Patty. How's that?

Another P.S.
Next week we begin night and day flying. That won't give me much

time to write but that's no reason you shouldn't.

Love
Skip

I received your card from Export and was (Oh there is my call) you weren't there. Only Joe was there. I told him to tell you I called. Couldn't talk too long. It amounts to a small fortune.

Love
Skip

Feb. 12, 1943
Roswell, New Mexico

Darling,

I did get your letter and Valentine and such a lovely one. The verse I treasure and always shall. Didn't answer sooner as things aren't going as well as they should. I'm not at all satisfied with my work. However I did receive a little encouragement today – was told to order my officers uniform, that of course doesn't signify that I'm as good as in – eight more weeks is a mighty long time. If I do get through I'll owe most of it to you – your letters go a long way in helping more than you realize.

I hope you understand when I tell you I'm not myself today. Just not in the mood for anything. Besides it's about 11:00 P.M. now and I take off on the first mission tomorrow which is 7:00 A.M. I only fly one mission a day this week, that's a break, anyway.

Love
Skip

Chapter 3 – 1943

Feb. 26, 1943
Roswell, New Mexico

Jo Darling,

As much as I'd love to discuss the subjects of love and marriage – I feel that I shouldn't. My reasons, though to you may appear paradoxical and one-sided are honest ones. You must admit without a doubt that at the present I am in no position to ask you to marry me. You take it rather hard now – can you imagine what you would feel like were I your husband? You are optimistic though, thinking of us – after the war – why I know without anyone telling me different that I'm living on borrowed time even now. But there is something about it that gets me – the excitement and exhilaration that comes with that ever present challenge of death. Soaring high above the clouds I glance at my companions in adventure – young men with a glint of laughter in their eyes, a sudden grin a meaningful gesture of the hand and the uncertainty that comes with men who challenge all the obstacles of the unknown. A feeling of warmth pervades my being I feel I belong – I know I belong I do belong!

I can't help but recall how easily you fitted into my life. Before I met you life to me was a game that I played according to my own set of rules. Live laugh and love for today without a thought of tomorrow to be or yesterdays that were. This simple philosophy worked exceptionally well till I met you. You fitted into my life so easily that from the very day we parted I knew I had lost something. I desire to see you again, speak to you again, hold you in my arms again. If it were a sexual emotion and the motivating force was one of passion it would be explicable. As you must know this is not true. You're all woman Jo and you know about these things than I do – should I intelligently and rationally seek the key to this problem or should I let things go on as they are and let nature take its course?

Love
Skip

Chapter 3 – 1943

March 10, 1943
Roswell, New Mexico

Darling,

I don't mind admitting you have really got me stumped. I thought I had you all figured out but that must have been pure imagination. You write of marriage and then come back and say you're sorry for doing so, why? You have every right to do so, besides I expect you to. I believe it's time we stopped kidding each other Jo, and faced the facts as they are. I asked for your opinion of this unique affair in my last letter. I must say you didn't offer much help. So up to date I'm still in a haze about everything and I suppose I'll remain in oblivion unless you come forth with some help in solving this problem. Do you think we should wait until this chaotic world is brought back to normal before thinking of marriage? Or should we grasp what few moments of happiness we can before it is, perhaps, too late? If it is the latter, you would have to be willing to come out here as chances of getting a leave upon graduating are practically nil. Darling I wish you wouldn't so shrewdly evade this issue as you have done in the past. It's vital that I know what you think. So until I hear from you I suppose I'll remain in a "fog."

Love
Skip

March 17, 1943
Roswell, New Mexico

Dearest Jo,

Received your letter and I sat down with the intention of writing a very long reply. I realize that it will be impossible to do so as there are things I know I can't write about – things that will make life more miserable and unbearable for the both of us. I never could talk you into anything and I suppose it would be foolish to commence trying.

So you want to become a WAAC – take a little friendly advice and stay the hell out. You don't know when you're well off. I can tell you that it's not what it's painted up to be. Don't let that Rah Rah stuff get the best of you – besides a woman's place is at home.

Thanks for the prayers kid. I certainly need them if anyone does. I only wish there was some way I could show my gratitude. Got to run along so I'll remain yours, till I can date up Hiro Hitos wife.

Love
Skip

April 8, 1943
Roswell, New Mexico

Darling,

The time is too short and precious trying to explain everything so I'll give you the facts as they are and I'm hoping things work out for the best. As you have probably anticipated, within a few days that <u>dream</u> is about to become a reality. Well I can't pat myself on the shoulder cause without your encouragement I know it couldn't be so. Seeing that you are responsible for my achieving what you may call success I can't see why you shouldn't be here to celebrate the same with me. To put it short and it's about time I used a little initiative, I'm expecting you here before the 17th. Don't you think I have the right to ask this of you? Don't say it's impossible cause I know it's not. I'll be patiently awaiting a wire as to the day you will arrive so that I can make arrangements accordingly. Irregardless of what path you may choose I want you to know that I'll forever remain at least your very best friend.

Chapter 3 – 1943

I wish you wouldn't write a letter saying you'll come or why with you it is an impossibility. For once do me a favor and send a wire stating simply either yes or no.

Love
Skip

Postmarked April 15, 1943
Roswell, New Mexico

Formal Invitation

The Roswell Army Flying School
Of
Roswell New Mexico
Announces the graduation of
Bombardier Class 43-6
Saturday morning April seventeenth
Nineteen hundred and forty-three
At nine o'clock

Post Theater

Postmarked April 25, 1943
Crawford Hotel
Carlsbad, New Mexico

Darling,

Just a few lines to let you know I've received your telegram and to let you know it make me feel good to know that you arrived safely. I'm staying at this hotel for a few more days as I don't start in to work until Monday. Miss you like only I can know. Write and let me know what everyone had to say.

Love
Skip

Student Det. C.A.A.F.
Carlsbad, NM

Postmarked July 8, 1943
Barksdale Field, LA

Dearest Jo,

Don't know whether to expect a reply to this little note or not, regardless I want you to know that I've arrived safely. I'm flying in the plane I anticipated I'd get – B-26. My stay here is indefinite, however I do know that this is my last phase before combat.

I'm not looking for sympathy when I tell you I know that I'm an awful heel. But please don't think to harshly of me and let it go at that – I mean don't take it out on friends of mine. I'm glad I got the opportunity to speak to you – I don't think I never would have forgiven myself if I hadn't. Because as cruel as it may appear to you, it so happens that I do love you. So until we meet again – or something be good and keep em smiling.

Love
Skip

Postmarked July 27, 1943
Barksdale Field, LA

Dearest Jo,

I know it is utterly useless to give an excuse for not writing immediately. If I did you wouldn't believe me. Jo I've always been frank with you. I want you to be the same. I take it from the way you act that I don't mean as much to you now as I did at one time – am I right? Well truthfully I can't blame myself too much because if I recall correctly I've told you at one time what an awful heel I really am. I myself thought that if anyone could alter my way of living it would be you – yes you've went a long way in daring so only I suppose the fault lies with me – perhaps I haven't met you half way or then again maybe I'm just a bad egg beyond repair.

Not much news around here except that they stopped building B-26's, can't get enough specialized pilots to fly them so I don't know what type of ship I may land in combat with. Have another cross country this coming weekend, but chances of going back to Pittsburgh are very slim. It will probably be in Chicago or Florida. Well, keep em smiling Butch.

Love
Skip

War & Navy Departments

11/15/43

V-Mail – Official Card

Season's Greetings from Great Britain

Love, Skip

Chapter 3 – 1943

Postmarked Dec. 4, 1943
12/5/43
N. Ireland

Dear Jo,

Haven't much to write about as I haven't heard from you as yet. Very possible that I'm a forgotten bad dream by now. As you can tell from this letter I'm in a very depressed mood tonite. It's getting so that anything someone suggests or does gets on my nerves. I know it is definitely wrong and yet I can't control myself. But I suppose there is very little I could tell you about myself that you don't know. At a time like this I like to be left alone with my thoughts. Tonite they are of you. Can't help but think that we could have gotten along swell with a little cooperation on my part. We all have our faults though, some of which can be overcome, others that can't. I wonder what your opinion was of mine? You know the old saying, "Absence makes the heart grow fonder", right now I'm inclined to believe it more so than ever. I am curious as to how you feel about everything. Do you think <u>ours</u> was a mere case of infatuation. Must you keep me in suspense much longer? I'm waiting patiently with a reply.

Love
Skip

P.S. Believe it or not but just now the radio is blaring out with Tuxedo Junction, and from Germany!

Postmarked Dec. 4, 1943
Somewhere in N. Ireland

Dear Jo,

By this time I suppose you've received my first letter. I honestly wish I knew whether or not you intend to send me a reply. Is it that your stubborn pride that won't permit you to do so, or have I hurt you beyond repair. I only ask you to give it a serious thought and I'm sure you'll agree that I've done the right thing. Then maybe all of this is a wasted effort. Perhaps by this time you've found a more exciting and enthusiastic playmate. Regardless I can't see a reason in the world why we shouldn't keep up a correspondence. I do ask one thing of you. If you don't care to write at least drop a card and let me know. I am interested in what the holidays will be like back home. Ours will be the same old thing – probably won't get a day off. Somehow it's hard to realize that I've left the good old USA. Things around here are rather dull. Nite life – what you can find of it consists of drinking beer in the so called "pubs". The "romance" angle has one advantage – it's dark out, so when you meet an Irish lass you hold hands and imagine you've another Grable. Being as my heart is well taken care of (Is it?) I find it impossible to pretend. I wish you'd let me know how long it takes for my mail to reach you. Well Butch here's hoping they end this damn war in a hurry so that we can once again lead a normal life. Take care of yourself and God Bless You.

Love
Skip

12/6/43

Dear Jo,

Here it is Saturday nite and believe it or not no headaches. Saturday nite was spent in a rather quiet way – listening to the radio mostly. And then of course along with sweet music comes the discussion of the fairer sex the boys have left back home. An affair such as that puts one in a very awkward position. I only have one comment to make and it ends there. Namely, "She may not be mine but she is the sweetest kid on this side of heaven with a heart of gold." Butch, I wish you would reply as to the way you feel towards me. Is it just a page in the past with no hope for the future? I ask you out of all fairness to you as well as myself. I've a few vital decisions to make and your reply has a lot to do with which way I decide. I don't know whether or not you know but my last leave in the states was shortened for the simple reason I wanted to avoid what happened previously – remember? Don't you think we've been influenced too much by different people? Do you think we should go on and hope for the best or drop the whole thing. I didn't intent to write of the above mentioned things but I find it impossible to write you and speak of the weather or something. Hoping you will see things my way. I'll be leaving you for now with loads of luck and the best of everything.

Love
Skip

P.S. Just found out that you people won't be able to write between the 6 and 25 of December so I'm beginning to wonder if I'll ever hear from you.

12/7/43

Dear Jo,

My last literary efforts probably sounded a bit dismal but I assure you it was only the temporary mood at that particular moment. All of us are in the very best of spirits and shall continue that way.

In my previous letters I've neglected to tell you anything of my travels after leaving the sates, until our arrival in North Ireland. We have visited Scotland and England. Though it was a short visit we had the sensation of having been through a world that is centuries old and has not undergone many changes. Our own Americans living in the modern U.S. can never appreciate these sentiments unless they travel as extensively as the members of the American armed forces today. One such a site is the Giant Causeway one of the seven wonders of the world. Only nature, herself, could build such a wonderful gateway.

Chapter 3 – 1943

Let's get back to my favorite topic, you! I really miss the sweet times we've had and hope the day isn't too far off when we may see one another again. Unless, of course, other interests may cause you to decide against that. Thinking of you and hoping I may soon be at your side.

Love
Skip

12/7/43

Dear Jo,

From the amount of letters you've been receiving from me I suppose you already know I've got loads of free time on my hands Writing you is time well spent. Of course, there is that everlasting doubt in my mind as to whether or not you will reply. I see but one outcome – I shall continue to write until I'm informed otherwise.

Just got back from one of these traveling USO shows. Consisted of two fellows – one a baritone the other the master of ceremonies. Six girls. (I take it for granted they were girls even though they appeared to be every bit of forty) made up the rest of the show. Oh yes the musical end of the show consisted of one piano player. The singing wasn't bad at all but this British sense of humor sure has me stumped. I've never heard so many dry jokes in my life. As a whole it was a very poor imitation of wit. You recall how I despised listening to An_____ over the radio well at the moment I wouldn't complain a bit.

Enough of England, once again let's get back to you! Just dying to know all about you. In reality it hasn't been so long but it seems like ages since I've seen you last. It wasn't on a very friendly basis was it? But I did get to see you and that was the main cause of spending that last leave at home. Are any of your brothers over here? If they are with their address it wouldn't be too much trouble getting in touch with them. Well I'm hoping your reply, if there is one reaches me in a hurry. So be good and God bless you.

Love
Skip

12/8/43

Dear Jo,

Here I am again with the same old complaint – no letter today. My mind tells me to give it up as a lost cause. But something down deep urges me to sit down and write at least a few lines. If I've judged you correctly, and I think I have, I don't think you would let a letter go unanswered. Though you can be very stubborn at times you are very easily influenced by people and can very easily be won over. Perhaps I did the wrong thing by writing to you – I only wish I knew. You see I've been told the best thing I could ever do would be to let you alone. This comes from someone both you and I know very well. So you can readily see why I'm so anxious to hear from you. Do you think it possible at all for us to be back on the same terms we were at one time?

Butch, I didn't want to write what follows but it seems to me that I must. At least in one sense I know I'll feel better. You certainly can recall my last leave. Remember me asking to marry you? If I ever meant anything I did that. Only one person knows that I've spoken the truth that's Mom. Before I left, the same morning, I explained everything to her adding of course the fact that I've been refused. Well anyway there wasn't much she could do but let me work things out for myself. Well I couldn't face it so I left. But that's all past history. Now I wonder what the future holds in store for me? Still waiting.

Love
Skip

12/10/43

Dear Jo,

It has finally happened, I've received my first letter from the good old States. It was from my people. Although I cherish the letter with all my heart, I was rather disappointed as I expected word from you at the same time – if not sooner. I guess it's futile to go on wishing so I'll try my best to forget the sweetest of memories I've had in my life and the girl who made them possible. I trust you're doing what you think best so I've no complaint to make whatever. After all wasn't it I who said that a woman's a fool for waiting for a soldier who is on foreign soil? Well I guess there isn't much more to say excepting that if I'm ever in a position to offer you any help of any kind I wish you wouldn't hesitate to ask. I'd be only too willing. Let's be the best of friends, shall we. Wishing you the best of luck in the world and God Bless You.

Your very best friend,
Skip

Not dated
Postmark unreadable

Dearest Jo,

Would love to get a few points cleared up now that the time is so short. But before I say anything I do want to remind you of one eve quite some time ago – Remember me telling you that regardless of what happens I'll always love you. You know as well as I did that, that was from the very bottom of my heart and still is. I also mentioned that in time that love can change to hate – Has this happened on your part? If it hasn't please let's stop being childish about this affair and act like grown-ups. If it has well that's simple enough, I just don't receive a reply. Regardless of what way you have chosen – I wish you the "bestest" of the best.

Love
Skip

P.S. You know I didn't mean what I said about making you miserable.

"Pistol Packin'Mama"
Most of Skip's 65 combat missions were flown in this plane.

Chapter 4
1944

Chapter 4 – 1944

1/1/44
APO, NY

Dearest Jo,

This being New Year's Day, I must confess my thoughts were of you. To me the New Year has done wonders already – I've received your Christmas card, which is the first piece of mail I've received from you. I take it you are in the very best of health. The address was quite a mess but it managed to get here. Upon reading the verse I couldn't help but ponder over the line "thoughts will be there with you", can it be that you do care regardless of what has happened? Here I go again hoping against hope! I do want to thank you for the card, it was very sweet of you.

I don't suppose there is any point in complicating things any more than they are but before bidding you adieu I do want to wish you the happiest of birthdays and the very best of everything. It is Jan. 11, isn't it?

Love
Skip

March 30, 1944
APO, New York

Dear Jo,

Received so many of your letters today, I hardly know where to begin. You build up my hopes in one only to knock them down in another. Regardless, I'm glad you've written – takes quite a load off my chest. You appear to stress one point in particular in most of your letters – the future as far as you and I are concerned. That is rather a touchy subject to discuss – from my point of view anyway.

Mostly so because I wonder if there is something to look forward to.
As you must know I've been more or less a fatalist in civilian life –
there's no question about it now. In my opinion one must be that way
to remain in this racket. Believe me things are far from being dull.

I've been on quite a number of missions over enemy territory. At
times we encounter no opposition but then there are times when
things get plenty hot. I am thankful to be flying in the same plane I
had been back in the states. When on pass we usually take in London.
So you see things move at rather a fast clip around here.

Judging from your letters you're a pretty busy young lady – never a
dull moment. No small wonder you've been having trouble with your
foot. I'm certain a week's absence from dances would kill you and
I'm certain it would do the leg a world of good (I sincerely hope it
gets well). I know this hardly makes up for all the mail I've received
from you – Perhaps the sun will shine tomorrow thereby turning my
fancy to thoughts of love and you – then I'll pick up my pen and rave
on some more.

> Love
> Skip

May 17, 1944
APO NY

Dearest Jo,

Your letter of May 2nd brought back loads of wonderful memories.
Silly ? -- -- Some of them yes, but unforgettable. When I stop to think
over the past I'm only sorry we didn't have more moments alone.
Times when words were of so little value and nothing mattered
excepting the idea that we two were together. I can't help write like
this for I wonder if it will be possible to regain at least a part of what
we have missed.

Chapter 4 – 1944

It was nice of Jane to try and let you in on the know. But I can't understand where she gets all this wonderful information. Were it true that I should get to go home after twenty-five missions -----I would have been home quite some time ago. Up to date (I'm knocking on wood.) I've got in over thirty missions. Quite a number EH! Not so much when you stop to consider that our operational tour of duty <u>was</u> fifty. May I add that at the present it appears as though I'll be here for the duration. However some of the boys are getting to go home. Lucky Stiffs! So keep your fingers crossed there is a speck of hope left.

When did this love affair between Jane and Walt begin? Will wonders never cease? And Jane being nervous just at the sight of his mother --- She must have it bad. I can see that Olga is a true blue example of what a wife should be – She will stay with him through thick and thin to the very end.

You know I'm not especially in love with Joe (the fat man) myself but don't you think he's right in trying to promote business? The only way to do it is to get the suckers to buy. And as for that place going to hell—I don't believe you've seen anything. The place wouldn't compare to some of the dens of iniquity around here.

It won't be much fun spending a well earned vacation at home – Why not take a little trip somewhere just to get away from the hum drum of city life. It would do you loads of good.

Not much of anything new goes on here—the old daily routine of army life goes on and on. I have stumbled into a bit of fortune a little while back—May 6th to be exact. It took a little over a year but my promotion from 2nd to 1st finally came through. Nothing exciting about it excepting that it means a few more shekels to spend towards a good drunk.

Before fading away I do want to tell you that I certainly appreciate your writing me every so often. I suppose I really should write more often – but then what could I say? Were I to tell you what I honestly think of this whole damn mess, the letter would never reach you. The thought of you is as good a luck charm as I ever want, after all it saw me through safely so far----I know it won't fail in the future. If some of the things in this letter don't make sense don't worry about it for I believe there are times when my mind goes blank and I don't know what I'm doing myself. Reminding you to keep the letters coming and I'll promise to write when time permits. Leaving you for the present with loads of LOVE.

Love
Skip

June 9, 1944
APO NY

Dearest Jo,

Glad to hear you enjoyed reading my letter although I can't see any reason for getting excited. I know you've received many a letter just like it. Sure is good to know you're well and getting along.

Before going on with this little note I'm going to ask you a favor. As you undoubtedly know your Sis has written to me – a very nice letter at that but at the present I can't for the life of me find time to write. So inform her that I haven't forgotten and I'll write at the next opportunity.

Getting back to you my dear I wonder if you know how much I do miss you? Come to think of it – it's ages since I've last seen you. Do you still have that merry twinkle in your eyes? Even as a baby it was there – well it was the first thing about you that attracted me. Tell me hon why did you put up with me all that time? I wonder if I've changed. You know Dear I may not be worth waiting for – just an old

Chapter 4 – 1944

nervous wreck. I don't think you'll recognize me when I can back. (Pretty sure about getting back aren't I)

Now that the second front has started how do the people back home feel? How did they take the news? Believe me the boys are all putting out every bit of effort to make this thing a success and with the spirit that prevails amidst all of us I know we can't miss.

Now for a little news as to what goes on here. I ran into a friend who is attached to the Air Corps in a round about way, namely George, known back home as "Gus". He claims to be one of your old dancing partners so I guess you know him pretty well. The old boy was so tickled at running into me that he insisted on having your address – I guess you'll be having more mail to answer shortly. Anyway now you've got someone who can keep an eye on me and to help keep me on that straight narrow path. Along with good news comes a little bad. I lost a very dear friend a little while ago who went down. A very jolly Irish lad who had been out with me a number of times. I went along as an escort to his funeral and I don't feel right since. Funny how low the value of life is during war time. The entire with which I come with from the States are in the very best of health. I've got well over forty missions in and still going strong. So you see things are moving right along. Speaking of Zup I've written to him several months ago and haven't as yet received an answer. I'm beginning to wonder with the invasion on there's no telling where he may be. If you should hear anything of his whereabouts, let me know.

Well Darling I've stretched this so called note into a lengthy novel. Probably cost you extra postage upon arrival. I'm kinda surprised at you though, no letter in a week and when it does get here not even a snapshot of yourself. You know I've quite a collection of pin-ups all of you but I would sure appreciate a few additions (PS Running out of ink.)

Here goes again: If the words aren't readable it's due to lack of sleep. I do want to remind you to keep writing cause you know that a letter from you means the world to me. Darling I miss you very much so much that it hurts. If only this damned bloody mess would end so that we could once more get together. So with an I Love You on my lips and you foremost in my thoughts I'll hit the bed.

Love
Skip

Oct. 12, 1944
APO NY

Dearest Jo,

Have been receiving your mail pretty regular and I'm sorry as hell I couldn't reply on time. I want to apologize, before going on, as I'll have to make this as brief as possible. Writing on one's knee by flashlight – with a little touch of wind just doesn't go well. It was sure good to hear that you're up and around again. And you better get real well but quick as I'm bound to come home <u>sometime</u>. I hope. Forgot to mention that I've been over in France sometime now. Just haven't got all the comforts of home we had in old England.

I suppose all the people back home are getting prepared for the holidays to come. As for ourselves we very often forget the day of the week. Once again I'm glad to hear that you're back on the upgrade, up and around.

As days go by conditions around here improve so that in the near future I may be in a position to write more often.

Love
Skip

NOTE:

Ladies diamond ring purchased on December 1, 1944 at Braun's
Jewelers in Braddock. Cost: $200.00
Receipt stamped: PAID

Skip flew three missions on D-day in this plane.
He carried this photo in his wallet his whole life.

Chapter 5
1945

Jan 2, 1945
(No envelope)

Dearest Jo,

Won't make any excuse for the shake in the writing as you know only too well the cause for it. Even at the present I'm wondering as to whether it's pure grain alcohol or "blended" trickling through my veins. However, I do believe that in a few weeks with the proper care I should be "fit as a fiddle". The trip down is a very painful subject to write of – imagine standing all the way from Washington to Richmond in something that was a very close resemblance to a cattle car. Believe me I was never so overcome with joy when getting off a train as last night.

I'm asking your forgiveness for the abrupt departure – but I always did despise those lengthy farewells – it appears to me as though they always lead to tears and before this whole mess is over heaven only knows we'll shed more than our share. It's only been one day but you're being missed something awful. If only we didn't have such a dim outlook on the future – and yet there must be millions like we two in the same predicament. We'll talk the thing over more thoroughly when I find out what the army intends to do with me. I'll be run through the usual routine beginning tomorrow. I understand my stay here will not exceed over two weeks, after that -------- ? I do hope that you're in the best of health and keep staying the same. Who knows I may call upon you with a very short notice – and if I find out that I'll be in the States at least six months, I can't see the point in waiting. Just as a reminder – You do know that all the running around didn't mean a thing it's you and only you I'm in love with! Will write more when I find what the score is till then.

All my love
Skip

P.S. Do you want to? My best to the family

Jan 16, 1945
Western Union Telegram – St Louis

Darling detained in St Louis for one day. Miss you. All my love. Skip

---

Jan 20, 1945
Western Union Telegram – Odessa Tex

Miss you. Letter follows. All my love. Skip

Jan 22, 1945
MAAF, Midland, Texas

Dearest Jo,

Now that I'm back in the States free time is a thing of the past. I won't tell you too much about Texas as you've rode through here before – believe me it hasn't changed a bit. In the few days that have passed I've found that I am not alone in more ways than one. The housing situation is something terrible. You can get a hotel room which is good for five days after that you must make room for someone else. I suppose we will have to wait till I can get a leave – that all depends on how long I have to go to school.

It's only been a little while back since I last saw you but already it seems like ages. I'm convinced that the only way I can be contented is being with you. Darling forgive the short letter but I'm still running around like mad drawing school books and other equipment. Miss you. Don't worry too much. We'll work this thing out together before long.

All my love
Skip

Jan. 28, 1945
Midland, Texas

Dearest Jo,

You've got me worried again dear – I hope that everything with you is just so. You see I haven't heard from you about a week now – You must admit that's quite some time. Anyway it seems like years. If I could only find some place to live I'd have you out here so fast your head would spin. I do have one hope – that is when the next class graduates – they send the fellows who are married elsewhere to instruct – that may possibly leave a few vacancies. If I don't get to see you darn soon I think I'll go absolutely <u>nuts</u>. I want you here by my side so that I can tell you how much I love you also by getting on your nerves – Did you know you are wonderful when you get angry? Yes I like you any way – even with your hair all up. Besides I could at least tell you if the seams in your stockings are straight or not – so you see I would be of some help.

Remember don't work too hard and oh yes see that you get to bed early these cold nights. Above all take care of yourself. Myself – I go to school five and a half days a week. Yesterday being Saturday, was spent in the <u>big</u> city of Odessa (10,000 pop) about 1/3 the size of Braddock, so besides the two theatres there really isn't much to do. I'm expecting to hear from you any day now if I don't I'll brain you.

All my love
Skip

P.S. Still want to?

Feb 1, 1945
Midland, Texas

Dearest Jo,

Nothing like starting the month off right. You know Butch I'm really
getting fed up with this sort of life. If you were around I'm sure things
would be different – I know for certain time would be no matter. As a
rule I always hate to admit I'm wrong – but this is one time I was –
why right now I should be a married man with no troubles outside of
making sure your seams are straight and rolls in your stockings are up
high when we go out. I do love you Butch everything about you. As
for another leave there is nothing definite – I can be here anywhere
from 6 weeks on up. I'm going to cut this short Darling as I've a few
more letters but before I started on them I wanted to remember you
first of all.

All my love
Skip

Feb. 6, 1945
Midland, Texas

Dearest Jo,

This place is certainly a madhouse tonight. Everyone is throwing their
two cents with into a pretty well heated argument. The reason for this
is the idea of the army making us go to school these long hours and all
the rest of this damn stuff we have to put up with in the army. Frankly
our morale as a whole is point zero. I don't think one of us would feel
bad if we were told that we were slated to go to combat tomorrow. So
if some words enter into this letter that don't belong there – sort of
skip over them as I'm getting into and out of this argument myself.
Anyway by the time tomorrow comes around we'll all feel better
again.

You certainly surprised me – in a very nice way – two letters in a week. Certainly helps a lot Darling. The best and only way to forget all of this is to think of you. If something doesn't happen to end this argument pretty quick I'll soon start getting the Brub Sight *[illegible]* into this letter.

Glad to hear you're getting enough time off these days – Good for your health you know. I'm trying my best to figure a way out of this – that is for the both of us – but everything is so damn uncertain around here. I can't figure just how this whole thing is going to end. I get into a funny mood and think of sending for you – if to marry you and send you right back – but that wouldn't be fair to the both of us. I suppose the only logical way is for me to get a leave after I'm through here and work fast once I get home. And believe me I'll try my best to get that leave – even if it means see the Chaplain. So I'll leave you for tonight Darling and get back into this queer argument as I'm in that mood myself. Miss you.

All my love
Skip

Feb. 9, 1945
Midland, Texas

Dearest Jo,

Intended to get this letter off in time so that it would put you in good spirits over the weekend. I know it won't get there in time but will do better in the future. So how have you been keeping the past few days? I do hope you're having more fun than I – no don't get me wrong it's much better than getting shot at. Anyway boiling things down to a fine point the only excitement one does have around this joint is one's wife but alas – that is something I am without – something must be done – some drastic measures must be taken to alter that situation. Darling you'll have to bear with me till the end of this month (if I can wait that long). By that time I ought to know how things stand. And by the way, don't worry your pretty little head about the cooking and

147

---- you know darn well you won't have time to boil water with me around – nine years is a lot of time wasted. I honestly can't see the point in wasting more. Remember – I'm the one who is in love with you and honestly dear I do miss you something awful.

Love
Skip

Feb. 11, 1945
Midland, Texas

Dearest Jo,

Here it is Sunday nite with nothing to do and even less to look forward to – that is as far as this place is concerned. I am becoming quite a movie fan these days – two movies in one day. One of these was a rip snortin wild west show with John Wayne – I believe more people got shot in the picture than we've lost in combat. Anyway the evening is being spent listening to recordings – only one drawback – you've got to wind the thing by hand so it gets pretty monotonous. When you get down this part of the country you'll see the excitement for yourself. Before this evening is over with I must get some "book learnin" as I have a two hour test tomorrow morning after which I must give a fifteen minute talk on any subject I wish to choose – I think I'll talk about my girl Jo. Only one thing wrong with that – it would certainly take more than fifteen minutes. Seriously though Jo I do hope you shall never tire of me. It appears as though you shouldn't – heavens you've put up with me for a long time even though it was on and off. If anything time has proven that we can get along despite the few quarrels – which I do admit were mostly caused by myself. Though you are stubborn at times I'm sure that will tend to make life just that much sweeter. I do wish you were here now. Wow I'd better stop thinking and wait until the day it becomes a reality! Incidentally you had better practice getting up early in the mornings – noon time is just a trifle late for the army. I must comment on your letter writing.

You've been doing wonderful even though I didn't get one over the weekend – I expect one tomorrow and I'm certain it will be here. Well be good – don't do anything I wouldn't and don't forget I do love you.

Love
Skip

---

13 Feb 1945
Midland, Texas

Dearest Jo,

Received bundles from home today – two letters and a Valentine Card all in one day – if you're not careful you'll spoil me again. The idea of this little note is not to offer any excuses as I don't believe any are in order. Anyway until you do receive the gift I had intended would reach you at Valentine's Day this will have to do. I do think that a few days patience on your part will pay dividends. Being as this is intended to be the card – some sort of poem should be order, being as I am not so inclined you'll have to settle for just a plain "I Love You".

I do not think that you are a doubting Thomas or any such thing but to give you a faint idea of what I along with the others are going through I'm sending this week's school schedule.

Well now I lay me down to sleep or something – No don't dream awhile of how nice it would be were you here.

Love
Skip

---

14 Feb 1945
Midland, Texas

Dearest Jo,

Happy Valentine's Day Butch. Tried to send a wire out it is impossible to send any holiday greetings due to the war. I'm just wondering as to what you do between my letters – appears as though I've acquired a habit or hobby – call it what you may – Would you say that was good or bad? Do remember letting me know that Sam got married. Well I wrote him immediately without knowing his address excepting of course that it was somewhere in Roswell. My letter found him and I did receive a reply. It's true enough. He is married and I do know the girl fairly well – a pretty slick chick. I think I'll get to see him next weekend as I'm asking for next Saturday off. At least it's a good excuse for a few drinks just for old time's sake. Of course I'm asking your permission – that is to have more than a few – Truthfully I haven't overindulged since I left home.

I suppose you're eating well these days being as I'm not around to bother you in any way – You'll have to forgive me though for I love to bother you for some reason or another. Only one answer, must be
Love
Skip

---

19 Feb 1945
Midland, Texas

Dearest Jo,

I just knew that you couldn't hold out much longer – no I'm not disappointed in you – I'm only glad you realize what a problem it is writing daily and try to make a half way decent letter – when I could say all I want in one sentence – I love you. Oh hell, I am angry in a way for I was hoping you'd receive my gift in time – but then that's very typical of Skip – always late. And I don't want you to think I'd forgotten about the earrings. It's just that I haven't the time for one thing and on the other hand there isn't too much to choose from. And I am glad to hear you're well Chesty. Do remember if I can write – you can too, even if you must pull your hair to fill up a page. Expecting to hear from you in the very near future.

All my love
Skip

---

15 March 1945
Midland, Texas

Dearest Jo,

Yes my hands were pretty much tied the past few weeks and then again I didn't have anything definite on the subject of leaves so I decided to wait until I did before writing. I've just finished six weeks, not seven as you thought and I'm scheduled to go through three more weeks of this (damn the luck). So you see I can't possibly make it home in time for the holidays. Better or worse yet I don't know when I'll get a leave. However after this three weeks is up and I happen to receive a half way decent assignment in a fair place I'll write for you and we'll get married wherever I happen to be stationed. As to whether you want to stay or not – I'm leaving that entirely up to you. As a suggestion you may take your vacation when I do write for you then if you can put up with me along with the State of Texas – well you just won't go back. Really rushed for time these days Hon so I'm cutting this short.

All my love
Skip

April 10, 1945
CAAF, Carlsbad, New Mexico

Dearest Jo,

No I haven't forgot how to write, it's just that things move so fast at times I never know what I night be doing from one minute to the next. Frankly I expected to be at home for Easter – what an awful letdown it was upon finding out that it was impossible. Things are quite a mess now – believe me – I am stationed here in Carlsbad instructing cadets. And as far as a leave is concerned – beats me. To be very frank with you if I weren't so financially embarrassed – that is if I could afford a hotel here (no ink) for a month or so I'd insist that you come down – but my hands are tied so what can I do. I never realized that getting married would be such a problem. And yet when I stop to think about it – I'd much rather we got married somewhere away from home. You can imagine the confusion we could avoid. I can't say much of this place that you don't know. You've been to Roswell – this is very much the same. It gets so bad at times we all feel like volunteering for another tour of combat duty and believe me were it not for you I wouldn't even hesitate. So if you should hear that I've done something silly – forgive me.

It's sure good to know that you're doing ok and not ill anymore. I know I'd feel just as well – were you with me – but by myself I feel I am at a loss. Looking forward to seeing you very much. Miss you.

Love
Skip

April 17, 1945
Carlsbad, New Mexico

Dearest Jo,

I don't know whether you remember or not – but today is an anniversary for me. Just two years ago the kid became a brand new shiny 2nd Lt. at Roswell – remember? And yet it really doesn't seem that long. Had you the nerve at that time it would have undoubtedly been a dual occasion – maybe triple – who knows? I do miss you Hon, and I sincerely believe if there is anyone who could keep me in hand – it's you. I'm disappointed as I was sure I'd get leave before going to work out here – but I guess that's out of the question. I feel awful at times. I suppose I never will amount to much – Yes I am in a very sentimental mood this evening – just looking at the new cadet class graduating brings back memories. If you don't darn soon find a solution to all this I suppose I'll go completely insane. In the present mood I see but one outcome – that I won't even mention as you've been hurt more than you deserve to be. You must forgive me but I just don't feel myself this evening – you see you are the only solution to all of my problems.

I'm going to ask a favor of you Hon, the picture enclosed was taken in Mexico and the only one we have – if you can get it enlarged <u>and</u> cleared up in spots I wish you would as my pal would love to have one – and besides I think it does me justice. A little on the nylons which should be on their way come tomorrow – I understand from people who have bought some they are good for one wearing – so don't be disappointed if they should run the first time you don them. And in your next letter I'm expecting to get a smell of the perfume – as much as I've heard of it – the aroma has never once filtered past me. So Chesty what else can I say excepting that I miss you an awful lot. Come to think of it I am pretty fortunate – gone all that time – and yet you did remain true blue when you know that you were free to do as you pleased. Maybe in the near future I can really show my appreciation.

Darling I'll leave you until tomorrow or will it be that long? I'm sure it won't. I didn't intend for this to be a novel but when I get in this mood there is just no stopping me. Miss you and you know I love you.

Love
Skip

153

29 April 1945
Officers' Club
Army Air Forces Bombardier School
Carlsbad Army Air Field, Carlsbad, New Mexico

Dearest,

Here it is another Sunday – but just another day – nowhere to go – nothing to do but sit and twiddle ones thumb while sopping up a few brews. I've seriously been thinking of asking you to come out here – but hell we can't stay in the sheet. Things should brighten up though – all of the non-combat personnel have to move by June 30 – that should leave some vacancies. If nothing works out I'll ask you to spend your vacation out here. Well we could get married and if prospects of finding an apartment were nil – I suppose you'd have to go back home – Then again maybe I could arrange to get leave at the same time. I've been thinking everything over and I hate like hell to cheat you out of anything.

I realize that just like any girl – you must have had dreams of getting married in a veil and at home. And there's nothing I'd like better than that. Oh why must there always be a but. If I do get leave it will be unexpected and for only so many days – hardly enough to do anything. All that trouble of inviting relatives and friends and then think of the arguments that are bound to arise. Were we to get married out here – no one would have anything to say. Believe me whoever said getting married is easy is all wet. And please Dear don't say whatever I do is ok. This is a 50-50 proposition – remember? Write soon.

All my love
Skip

12 May 1942 *[dated as 1942, but believed to be written in 1945]*
Carlsbad, New Mexico

Dearest Jo,

Received a number of your letters lately but I've honestly been rather busy. As a matter of fact at the present I do not know whether I'm writing American or Chinese. However before going on with trifles I do want to inform you of things which I do believe are very important as far as you and I are concerned. To begin with it is a definite and well established fact that yours truly will not get a leave prior to some time in the latter part of December. Well you realize what all that means waiting and all that – truthfully it's getting the best of me. If what you have said is true and you do have a vacation coming up – why for the love of Pete don't you spend it out here – then it would undoubtedly be indefinite – and we could both return for home together. I realize it will be kind of rough but people have had it a lot worse – haven't they. What I'm trying to say – damn it – if you are taking a vacation why not make it a good one so that we can get married and the hell with what the people think. You know darn well I'll never hold it against you – without a doubt it will be the very best thing that ever happened to me. If you do agree with me I expect you to send me a wire as to when you will arrive so that I can plan everything accordingly. If you don't well -- ? Who knows.

> All my love
> Skip

Afterword

Before reading these letters and cables, and considering that I'm one generation removed from the history, my understanding of this part of my family consisted of youthful memories of family visits. My grandmother, Pap Pap's sweetheart, died when I was very young. I remember a very sweet woman, hair in a beehive, wearing a blue-green dress. Kind, gentle, and accommodating, but there must have been some steel underneath to be my grandfather's wife. Or so I thought before I read the correspondence.

I did not know the Skip that my mother and my Uncle Joe know. For me he was a great big man with silver-white hair that would show up with quarters and dimes and nickels that he would pass out to the grandchildren after a stop in Las Vegas on the way to visit. For all I know, that and the clothes on his back were all that survived those stops in Vegas. Goodness knows he burned all of his luck over Europe. I also remember that he smelled of cheap cigars and aftershave and that he could not operate a remote control for the television. All this is to say that there is absolutely no accounting for what a young person will remember.

He was so young, ten years my junior at the beginning of the correspondence. Young men are interesting beasts, a banquet of confidence and moxie and sass that only youth can provide. Apparently Pap Pap wasn't shorted on his allotment of any of these traits. Time and experience consume our reservoir of these qualities, and hopefully it does not draw too deeply. Pap Pap's tone becomes almost fatalistic at times. It is clear from his notes that in the darkest times he looked to my grandmother to help stem the despair. At first she represented the hopeful fancy of a young man. Then she became the absolute focus of a man who has seen too much living and dying in too short a time. Too often, we realize what is really important too late. Thankfully for both them – and for us – they did in fact find each other.

But what kind of person does that experience create? A man can be many things: kind and gentle, brutal and hard, ruthless and aloof, mischievous and playful. He may rise to great heights or slink into historical obscurity. But when a man loves a woman, he becomes formidable. Separated by an ocean and war, when Pap Pap realized what he wanted and what he might have, his letters gained an urgency that only acute clarity can bring.

Other than being my grandfather and serving in WWII, I doubt any stranger would say there was anything especially spectacular or noteworthy about him. What we – all of us – need to remember is that what he did is, in fact, spectacular. The war became the organizing principle for the country and everybody in it. It was, through necessity of resources, all-consuming. But one cannot draft, order, or in any way blunt the feeling that a man has when he finds the woman who will matter to him. We knew the part of my grandfather that survived WWII, both as children and grandchildren. I am glad that I now know the part of my grandfather who loved a woman deeply. I have always been grateful to the people who fought in the war. It shaped much of the world I've known. But I admire the man who wrote these letters, and the love that he shared with my grandmother is the true legacy they gave to us.

Daniel Joseph Murphy

Grandson of Joseph "Skip" Skibinski